3,00

USED TO KILL

ALSO BY LILLIAN O'DONNELL

Pushover
A Private Crime
A Wreath for the Bride
A Good Night to Kill
The Other Side of the Door
Casual Affairs
Ladykiller
Cop Without a Shield
The Children's Zoo
Wicked Designs
Falling Star
No Business Being a Cop
Aftershock
Leisure Dying
The Baby Merchants
Dial 577-R-A-P-E
Don't Wear Your Wedding Ring
The Phone Calls
Dive into Darkness
The Face of the Crime
The Tachi Tree
The Sleeping Beauty Murders
The Babes in the Woods
Death of a Player
Murder Under the Sun
Death Schuss
Death Blanks the Screen
Death on the Grass

USED TO KILL

by

Lillian O'Donnell

G. P. PUTNAM'S SONS
New York

G. P. Putnam's Sons
Publishers Since 1838
200 Madison Avenue
New York, NY 10016

ISBN 0-399-13782-3

Printed in the United States of America

USED TO KILL

Chapter ONE

She got the call from her agent at the last minute. A unit of Global Films was shooting a Pepsi commercial in Bermuda. One of the models had come down with severe facial dermatitis. Obviously, she couldn't work. Could Joyce go down right away? She could. It was the excuse to get away that she'd been looking for. She took it as a good omen.

Her plane was the last one to land before the airport closed and the storm hit. Actually, the storm veered at the last moment and all the island got was the backlash. According to the locals, it wasn't much of a storm; it didn't even qualify as a hurricane; they called it a *disturbance*. But Joyce had never seen anything like it. She sat in her hotel room through the night and as she watched the wind lashing the palm trees, churning the ocean, driving the rain in sheets, she was possessed by an inner turmoil. It wasn't till dawn, when the storm finally showed signs of abating, that she stumbled into bed. By then she was covered with sweat.

She woke a few hours later to a sunny, breezy day. The air was fresh. Everything had that scrubbed look typical after a violent storm. She felt cleansed, too.

* * *

Two days after the disturbance grazed Bermuda, storm warnings went up in Florida and along the eastern seaboard. The hurricane season had officially started, but no one expected anything serious so early in June, especially not in New York City. Nevertheless, the storm was heading in that direction and was gathering strength. The entire tristate area was under a storm watch. Though the sun was shining in a nearly cloudless sky, the storm, christened Adele, continued to pick up speed. It was scheduled to hit the metropolitan area sometime in the late afternoon of Wednesday, June fifth. Weather reports were so emphatic that most companies were sending their employees home at lunch time. But Rachel Montrone's boss was out of town and he would expect her to be at her desk and available.

She had lunch sent in. Afterwards, she went to the washroom for a cigarette. Smoking was off-limits everywhere else, and though she was alone, it didn't occur to Rachel Montrone to break the rule. She smoked the cigarette down to the stub, inhaled the last drag deeply, and ground it out. A spray from a pocket-sized vial of her favorite scent dispelled any trace of nicotine. She surveyed herself in the mirror. She had just passed her forty-fourth birthday, but she decided she didn't look it. The five or six pounds she'd put on recently were actually becoming; the extra weight plumped up the fine lines at the corners of her pale blue eyes. The new, bouncy hairstyle helped, too. She was still attractive and had plenty to offer—to the right man, she thought. Satisfied, she stepped into the corridor and headed back to her office in the executive suite. The phone on her desk was ringing.

She made a lunge for it. The receptionist had left and she wanted to pick it up before the recording kicked in.

"Triad Paper. Mr. Trent's office." She was out of breath.

"What took you so long?"

"Sorry, Mr. Trent. I just stepped outside."

He started to ask why one of the other secretaries couldn't have answered but had no time for petty details. "I wanted to let you know I'm coming back a day early. I'll be in tonight."

"You're not going back to Toronto?"

"No."

"They're predicting a hurricane is going to hit New York."

"I know. I'll be coming from the other direction. I expect to beat it, or slip in behind it. Is Maurice in?"

"He's at the beach house."

"Still?" Maurice Jessup was Douglas Trent's business partner. It was policy that one of them should always be present at the main office, but only a week ago an ocean storm, not a hurricane but destructive enough, had hit the Virginia Beach community where Jessup had property. He'd gone to check the damage.

"Well, get hold of him and ask him to come back right away," Douglas Trent instructed. "I need to see him first thing tomorrow morning."

"Yes, sir." Rachel Montrone could visualize the scowl on her boss's dark, broad, brooding face. "Is everything all right?"

"Everything's lousy," he retorted. "But it can be fixed."

"Yes, sir."

It was the current custom for everyone, from executive secretary to junior typist, to call the boss by his first name. Rachel Montrone had joined the company nineteen years ago when such familiarity was unheard of. Now secretary to one of the partners, her position and her many years of service certainly entitled her to do the same, but she considered it unsuitable. It irked Rachel when some insipid file clerk in a tight skirt wiggled into the office crooning *"Good morning, Douglas"* as she delivered the ritual coffee.

"And get in touch with the accountants," Trent continued. "Tell them to have one of their people in here at ... say, eleven A.M."

"Anything else, sir?"

"No, I don't think so. That's it for now."

"Would you like me to notify Mrs. Trent of the change in schedule?"

He hesitated. "Tonight's her late night at the studio, isn't it?"

"That's right."

"So she wouldn't be available anyway. Let it go."

"Yes, sir. Shall I send a car to the airport to pick you up?"

Again he was uncertain. "Well ... no. I don't know what plane I'll be on. I'll be going straight home; a taxi will be fine. See you in the morning, Rachel."

Hurricane Adele came up the coast with one hundred mile an hour winds and pounding surf. Having inflicted new damage on areas hit just a week before, it veered out and spent itself at sea. New York City and the coastal areas of Long Island, Connecticut, and New Jersey were left unscathed. There the night of June fifth was a balmy preview of summer.

Her tap-dancing class ran late. By the time Emma Trent changed out of her practice tights and made it to the movie theater around the corner, the last show had already started. She bought a ticket and went in anyway. It was after midnight when the movie let out, but nobody was in much of a hurry to go home. The crowd lingered in front of the theater, laughing, chatting, and sharing the pleasure of what was turning out to be the summer's blockbuster attraction. Because it was midweek and with graduation approaching, there were few teenagers; they had better things to do, even including studying. Senior citizens, having taken advantage of the special afternoon matinees, were home. The crowd consisted largely of middle-aged couples, and Emma Trent knew many of them. Some were her neighbors, others parents of her pupils. They greeted her. She responded. As the marquee lights were turned off, the crowd began to disperse. Some headed for the King George on the corner of Austin Street for a late snack.

"Care to join us, Emma?"

That was Tony Hillyard. He and his wife, Athena, were parents of one of her most talented ballet students. "Not tonight, thanks."

"When is Douglas due home?"

"I expect him tomorrow."

"I guess you'll be glad to have him back."

"I certainly will."

"Hey, Teach! Want a ride?"

That was Buzz Grogan, athletic coach at Jamaica High. She owed a large part of the success of her dance studio to Grogan's support. Emma Trent was a dancer. She loved ballet, but she'd never had the money or the opportunity to get the intensive training which might have qualified her for one of the prestigious troupes—the Joffrey or the American Ballet Theater. She had been able to get work in the chorus of the road company versions of a couple of Broadway hits. In between she'd worked in the line in Vegas. She got the jobs more on the basis of her looks than her abilities. She was realistic enough to know that and to realize that her looks wouldn't last forever.

When Douglas Trent proposed, she accepted, and for a while they were happy. One of the problems was that she didn't have enough to do. Then one day she read an article in the *Times* titled "Dance for Team Athletes." It recounted how members of Dartmouth College's sports teams were improving their skills—in the ballet studio. Football, hockey, soccer, baseball, and basketball players were participating in ballet classes and finding applications to their own sport through ballet techniques. Emma Trent was excited. Here was a chance to use her skills, to have a life of her own in dance. Offering such a discipline to college students was one thing; to convince local high schoolers was another. She decided to approach it obliquely—through the girls. She went to Grogan, told him she was considering opening a dance studio and offered to instruct the girls' basketball team for free. On the basis of what she could accomplish with them, she wanted the opportunity to work with the boys' teams.

She'd gotten it, and from there went on to open her own studio. Now both the girls' and boys' teams were at the top of their respective leagues. Grogan went around beaming and taking credit for discovering Emma. The principal and the PTA were happy, particularly because Emma hadn't asked for money. She didn't need to. Her reputation was attracting as many pupils as she could handle.

Grogan was a big, burly, red-headed Irishman. If anyone had told him a couple of years back that he'd be advocating ballet training for his athletes, he would have choked laughing. His wife, Kate, a diminutive woman with dark brown hair and a white skin marred by a spidery web of fine lines though she was not yet thirty-five, had been against the venture. Now, she admitted publicly that she'd been wrong. Privately, she was still not convinced.

"Car's just around the corner, Teach," Grogan said and placed a guiding hand on each woman's elbow.

Emma Trent was twenty-three, tall, long-legged, with a firm dancer's build. She wore tailored beige linen slacks cinched tightly to show off her tiny waist. She had long, silky light brown hair. Worn loose, it fell around her shoulders like a shawl; when she tied it back, it showed off her flawless complexion, her liquid, amber eyes, and perfect profile. Her looks, however, were not always an asset. Women often resented her because of them. She knew Kate Grogan was wary of her.

She hesitated. "No," Emma Trent decided. "No, thanks. It's a nice night. I think I'll walk."

Grogan frowned. "I'm not sure that's a good idea."

"If you're referring to 'the slasher,' they've got him. He's locked up. It's all over."

Recently there'd been a series of attacks on women in the area. In fact, the assailant had waited on this very block, at the subway entrance on the corner of Queens Boulevard, looking for a likely victim—anyone heading away from the bright lights and the crowds toward the Gardens, a section of expensive homes set in well-tended grounds on tree-shaded streets. He stalked his prey till she was alone and then he moved in and plunged a small knife into her back, stabbing repeatedly. While he hadn't killed anyone, he had certainly inflicted serious injury and trauma.

"Still..." Grogan shook his head.

"We've increased the neighborhood patrol," Emma pointed out. "And if that's not enough for you..." She opened her handbag and let each peer inside.

"Mace?" Kate Grogan whispered. "That's illegal here."

"I know. But I'd rather pay a fine than get cut."

They parted. Emma Trent crossed the street and passed under the arches into Station Square. This was the start of the Gardens enclave. Following Greenway North, she turned on Clinton Place, a dead end serving four stately homes, each set on professionally landscaped grounds. As she had said, it was a fine night. It was hard to believe that a few hours ago they had been under the threat of a hurricane.

Up ahead, the Trent house, a broad, three-story French Normandy—style edifice of white painted brick with aqua shutters, glowed serenely in the moonlight. Its privacy was provided by a high hedge of taxus yews. Emma stopped short at the gate between the yews. Except for the lanterns on either side of the front door, which were controlled by an automatic timer and were lit, the rest of the house should have been dark. But there were lights on on the second floor in Douglas's room. He wasn't supposed to be home till tomorrow, she reminded herself. He could very well have finished his business a day early and not bothered to advise her. That wouldn't be unusual. Emma felt her stomach tighten and a wave of nausea.

Should she call the private security force? Should she get one of the neighbors to go in with her? Emma Trent looked at the other houses on Clinton Place. They were all dark. Everybody had gone to bed. Taking a deep breath, she marched up to the front door and put her key into the top lock, the dead bolt. It was engaged—as she'd left it when she went out. Douglas, once inside, would have relocked it. Good.

She entered quietly and pulled the door shut but did not lock it, in case she needed to get out quickly. She stood there, not moving, not turning on any lights, barely breathing, only listening. Then, still in the dark, she called.

"Douglas? Is it you?"

No answer.

Now she flicked a switch and a small, crystal chandelier threw shards of light on a spacious black-and-white marble foyer. Another switch and wall sconces illuminated a staircase curving gracefully toward the second floor. She went to the foot and called up once more.

"Douglas?"

She listened for the telltale sounds that might betray an intruder, but the house remained silent. From her handbag Emma Trent took the Mace she had proudly displayed to the Grogans, but she didn't get much confidence from it. Still, she clutched it tightly and with her other hand turned on the lights in the living room. Everything appeared normal. Back across the hall she proceeded to the dining room, then to the pantry, turning on lights as she went. It was in the kitchen that she found what she'd both expected and dreaded—evidence of a break-in. The glass of the top panel of the kitchen door had been smashed. A trail of ground glass led her along the rear hall to the den.

The safe had been blown open. Without taking time to see what had been taken, she returned to the front of the house. For a moment she stood at the foot of the stairs and then, silently, she climbed up to the second floor, turned left to the room whose lights she'd seen from the street. The door was ajar. She stepped inside.

Douglas was huddled in a far corner, on his knees, both arms raised to shield his head. He was covered with blood. There was blood everywhere. She had never seen so much blood. She felt the gorge in her throat rise. Knowing she was going to vomit, she rushed for the bathroom.

But it was even worse in there. There was blood on the floor, on the walls; the tub was ringed with it. Swallowing and tasting bile, she turned, and in her rush to get out tripped and fell, and threw up right there. Still retching, she managed to get on her feet and was on her way to her own room to call the police before it occurred to her to wonder what had caused her to stumble.

Chapter
TWO

For the past six weeks, while the slasher terrorized the neighborhood, the men and women of the Yellowstone Boulevard Station had rested very little. With the perp apprehended, they were just beginning to relax and get back to a normal routine when the call from Clinton Place was routed through to them. The first pair of RMP (Radio Motor Patrol) cars responded in under four minutes. They were met at the door by the victim's wife, Emma Trent. Wan and shaken, Mrs. Trent directed them to an upstairs bedroom but herself remained behind, clinging to the newel post.

One look sufficed Officers Al Yardney and Jerry Gardner. By the time they were joined by two more RMPs, Yardney and Gardner had already advised Communications to make the standard notifications relating to a homicide. As the word went out, more cars, marked and unmarked, converged on Clinton Place. Detectives, crime-scene specialists, forensic and photographic units and, of course, someone from the Medical Examiner's Office, responded. At first, the neighbors ignored the sirens and flashing lights. New Yorkers were accustomed to disturbances in the night, but this was too much to sleep through. Windows were raised at last and, after a while, lights were turned on.

Homicide detectives didn't routinely work the grave-
yard shift. Though the city's average homicide rate had
risen by a staggering twenty-six percent and most of the
murders admittedly occurred after midnight, they were
usually of an unsophisticated nature—results of family
altercations, drug related, mob rubouts—which a detective working out of the precinct squad was deemed qualified to handle. Officer Al Yardney was smart enough
and had been around long enough to sense this one didn't
fit the ordinary. For one thing, it had occurred in a privileged neighborhood, one well protected by its own security force. At the same time, these people were not
strangers to violence. Maybe bullets didn't fly at random
on these private streets, but the slasher had stalked his
victims here only recently. The notorious "Son of Sam"
had killed in this enclave of privilege. The people in these
houses remembered.

After a brief inspection of the premises and a brief,
cautious and courteous interrogation of the victim's wife,
Yardney requested someone from Homicide.

During regular hours, Communications would ring
Queens Homicide and whoever happened to pick up the
phone would "catch the squeal." After midnight, the
operator referred to an "on call" list, first trying someone
who lived near the scene. Sergeant Raymond Dixon's
name was at the top of the list and he was at home—as
usual since he and Patty had split up.

Among the cops who were his buddies, the reaction to
divorce was either a wild outbreak of carousing and wom-
anizing, or withdrawal and introspection. That was what
had happened to Ray Dixon, and it was ironic because
before the divorce he'd never been in a hurry to come
home. He wasn't unfaithful; he didn't play around; he
didn't hang out with the guys. There were no quarrels between him and his wife, rather a chill politeness that was
much more painful and a chasm much harder to bridge.

Ray Dixon was thirty-two, neither young nor old for a detective sergeant. He could remain that rank for the rest of his career, but also there was plenty of room to rise—and Ray was ambitious. He was six feet tall, with wavy, dark brown hair already threaded with gray, an aquiline nose, and full lips. His manner was quiet. Whenever possible he kept in the background so that when he did take command his forcefulness was that much more startling and effective. Women were very much attracted to him, but he didn't seem to be aware of that. All his life, as far back as he could remember, there had only been one girl for him, Patty Foley. Patty had been his schoolmate, his childhood sweetheart, and finally his wife. It wasn't till they were married that he realized they were strangers.

Patty either couldn't or wouldn't understand his needs, his dedication to the Job, or his desire for family. She couldn't take the stress of being a cop's wife. She worried constantly, and expected him to call in all the time.

He couldn't live within the limitations of her fears or help her in overcoming them. She refused to give him a child. If anything should happen to him, she argued, if he was killed or injured, she didn't want the added burden of raising a child by herself.

They agreed finally that they had no future together.

In the settlement, Patty got the house, which had been too big for just the two of them, anyway, and which she would now sell. Ray moved into a furnished studio in a characterless building on Queens Boulevard near the Queens Boro Hall and Criminal Courts complex. Surely the fact that it had all been so quick and amicable indicated they hadn't truly loved each other? he asked himself over and over in the lonely hours. If they had truly loved each other, wouldn't they have tried harder to make it work?

He was in his robe and slippers reading the self-allotted

chapter of *From Beirut to Jerusalem* when the call came. He made a note of the address, then jumped into his clothes—the standard outfit for such occasions, chinos, brown plaid shirt, loafers. He strapped on his shoulder holster and police special and a summer-weight brown cord jacket. He checked in the mirror, not to see how he looked, but to make sure the gun was properly seated and didn't show. Some cops didn't care, in fact preferred, that it should. To each his own, Dixon thought.

His car was parked at the back of the building. To his way of thinking, getting it out of a garage would result in time wasted. On the other hand, keeping a nice car on the street risked vandalism and theft. So Dixon drove what looked like a jalopy: an '88 Pontiac Bonneville with fifty-nine thousand miles on it, left front fender dented, chrome rusted and pitted, one door replaced, nonmatching. But under the hood everything was in prime condition. It started at the first turn of the ignition key and stopped at the touch of the brake. Within twelve minutes of getting the call, Detective Sergeant Ray Dixon entered the house on Clinton Place.

"What've we got?" he asked Officer Yardney.

Albert Yardney was older and had been on the Job longer, but was still riding motor patrol. He would have liked to make detective, but that was as much a matter of luck as it was ability, of making a big bust or catching the attention of the brass. He was not without ambition, but perhaps he was a little too comfortable. It showed in the extra pounds on his hips. But he could move when he needed to and he was a shrewd observer. At Dixon's question, he flipped open his notebook.

"The victim is Douglas Trent, a partner in Triad Paper Company. He was away on a business trip and came home unexpectedly, according to his wife. Apparently, he was alone in the house."

"Where's the wife?"

Yardney nodded toward the living room where Emma Trent sat at one end of the sofa staring vacantly into space. Dixon considered for a moment, then shook his head. "Later." He started up the stairs to the second floor.

It seemed to Ray Dixon that the more violent the crime, the more brutal and lacking in respect for humanity, the more men and women whose job it was to deal with it indulged in black humor, shielding themselves with boisterous exchanges. But there was little here tonight, he noted, standing at the threshold of the murder scene.

It was a large and expensively decorated room, Dixon registered peripherally. What stunned him was the amount of blood, an arterial gush that appalled him. Plus the almost pathetic position of the victim. It wasn't easy to look. Dixon didn't know any cop who ever found it easy. To interpret what had happened and to understand it, you had to look at the condition of the victim long and hard and make sure you didn't miss anything. He moved in closer. Douglas Trent was on his knees, huddled in a corner, arms frozen in position as he had tried in vain to deflect the lethal blows. From what Dixon could tell, he had been beaten repeatedly, long after he'd stopped resisting. Douglas Trent had been beaten about the head, one side of his skull crushed.

"You think you've seen it all," Don Fletcher murmured at his shoulder.

Dixon turned. Fletcher was one of the bright young recruits the new Chief Medical Examiner had brought in to reorganize a department that had recently come under heavy criticism. Fletcher was a keen pathologist and an enthusiastic proponent of forensic training for every cop who had business at a crime scene. Dixon was surprised to see him. His presence indicated the homicide was already being perceived as out of the ordinary.

"Can you give me an approximate time of death?" he asked.

"Rough guess—three or four hours ago." Fletcher believed in sharing what he knew.

"He's a big man, well nourished and fit," Dixon observed. "Unless he was either drunk or drugged, I'd say it took more than one assailant to do this to him."

"Right."

"What about weapons?"

"Bats, or heavy slabs of lumber."

Dixon frowned. Not items housebreakers were likely to be carrying around unless they expected to use them. He looked inquiringly at Yardney.

"No, haven't seen anything like that, Sarge. Of course, we haven't really looked."

So now the three of them made a visual sweep of the room and Dixon noted details he hadn't bothered with before. The furniture was dark mahogany, the carpet light blue wall to wall; bedspread and drapes, dark blue and severly tailored. No vanity table, no toiletries on the bureau. A man's room. On the far side near the closet he noted two suitcases, one standing on its side, the other on a luggage rack. Both were unlocked. The one on the floor was empty, the other contained shirts, shorts, ties, and used linen rolled up in a ball. He opened the closet. Expensive suits hung on a rod, neatly arranged according to color.

Dixon reasoned aloud: "Trent had returned from his trip and started to unpack, but he was interrupted." He examined the carpet at the closet area but found no marks. "Maybe he heard a noise downstairs and went to investigate." He acted it out. "He got as far as the door? Maybe the landing? Anyway, the perps met him and pushed him back, beating him, till there was nowhere for him to go, till he was cornered and on his knees." A trail of dark stains confirmed the reenactment.

But there was another set of tracks that led to the bathroom.

"Somebody took a shower!" Dixon exclaimed. The shower head still dripped and there was a rusty residue in the tub.

"It looks that way," Fletcher agreed.

Dixon came out. "And somebody threw up."

"Mrs. Trent," Yardney told him.

"Right." He stared at the pile of vomit.

Fletcher waited. "Well, unless there's something else . . . ?"

"No, no. Thanks, Doc. You go ahead."

Once the body was gone, it was always a lot easier to be impersonal, Dixon thought, a lot easier to deal with the terms of motive and opportunity.

"How did they get in?" he asked Yardney.

"Broke in through the kitchen."

Yardney led the way down the backstairs, through the pantry and into the kitchen. The door was equipped with a standard self-closing lock and dead bolt. Neither lock was engaged, but the door had a large glass panel that was smashed. All the intruders had to do was reach in for the door knob.

"You'd think people would be more security-conscious nowadays," Dixon muttered. He wondered if the noise of the breaking glass could have been heard by Douglas Trent all the way upstairs. He made a note to be sure the door was dusted for prints.

Now it was time to interrogate the victim's wife.

Emma Trent was still sitting where Ray Dixon had seen her—on the living room sofa, back straight, eyes unfocused, hands clasped tightly in her lap. He walked over and stood in front of her. She didn't look up. In shock, he thought.

"Mrs. Trent? I'm Sergeant Dixon." He showed her his ID. "I'm very sorry for your loss. I regret having to disturb you at this time, but there are some questions I have to ask and if you could answer them, it would help a lot."

She had a perfect oval face without even a trace of lines. Her hair was light brown, long and silky. Her amber eyes were limpid. Nothing flashy about her, Dixon thought, but the longer you looked, the more you were struck by her beauty. She had to be at least twenty years younger than her husband, and she didn't belong in this gloomy room with its dark paneling and heavy drapes and massive furniture.

Emma Trent came back from wherever she'd been and focused on Dixon.

"He wasn't supposed to be back till tomorrow." She spoke so softly he had to step closer and lean down to hear. "That's why I went to the movies. I wouldn't have done that if I had known he was coming home. I would have been here, if I had known. I would have been here waiting," she repeated almost like an incantation.

"Where had he been?"

"In Toronto. On a business trip. Douglas is a partner in Triad Paper. Was a partner," she moaned. "If only he'd called to let me know."

"What time did you leave the house, Mrs. Trent?"

"Early this afternoon. Around two. I have a dance studio. Most classes are scheduled in the morning to accommodate the mothers, and after school for the children. Once a week I have a night class. On Wednesday. Tonight. I let it run a little late because everyone was doing so well and enjoying it so much."

"After the class you came straight home?"

"No. I went to the movies, to the theater around the corner. When I got there the last show had started, but

I went in anyway." She bit her lips; her eyes filled. "I was lonely. I didn't feel like coming home to an empty house. If I had come home ..." She didn't finish.

"What time did the movie let out?" Dixon asked.

She frowned. "After midnight. Around then. I'm not sure."

"No problem. We can easily find out. Did anybody see you after the show?"

She didn't appear to grasp the importance of the questions and replied in the same dispirited manner. "I spoke to several people. I don't exactly remember who." She raised one hand up to her eyes in a graceful gesture.

"They'll remember," Dixon assured her. "What time did you get home?"

"I spoke to the Grogans, Buzz and Kate." She returned to the previous question. "They offered me a lift, but I decided to walk. It was a nice night." She sighed heavily. "I strolled. I was in no hurry. It's only a short way."

Based on the movie, the time could be approximated, Dixon thought. According to Doc Fletcher's preliminary estimate, death had occurred between nine P.M. and one A.M. At this point, Emma Trent's alibi was loose. That didn't disturb him.

"All right, let's say you got in at about twelve-thirty. When you approached the house, did you notice anything wrong? What I'm getting at—was there any indication there had been a break-in?"

"The lights were on. I saw them from the street."

"Which lights?"

"Upstairs. The lights in Douglas's room."

"They weren't supposed to be on?"

"No. I told you I left at two in the afternoon. The house should have been dark except for the lanterns at the front door, which are activated by a timer."

"So what did you think when you saw the lights in your husband's room were on?"

"I thought he must be back from his trip."

"But he hadn't notified you."

"No."

He let it go for now. "So you saw the lights in your husband's room from the street. Then what did you do?" Many husbands and wives used separate bedrooms, Dixon mused, and it wasn't necessarily an indication the marriage was in trouble. A May-December union presented difficulties, but he had, at this time, no reason to assume they weren't being overcome. "When you came in, what did you do?" he repeated.

"I called, but Douglas didn't answer."

"Then what?"

"I took a look around."

"That wasn't very smart, Mrs. Trent. Didn't it occur to you that something might be seriously wrong? That someone might have broken in and the intruder could still be there?"

"It was . . . instinctive."

He sighed. "All right. Go ahead."

"That's all there is. I locked the front door."

"Was it unlocked when you came in?"

"No, it was locked. That was one of the reasons I thought Douglas must be back."

"And then?"

"I went upstairs."

"Did you turn on any lights along the way?"

"Naturally."

"Didn't you think it odd that your husband hadn't turned any lights on except in his own room?"

"It didn't occur to me."

"Did you call to your husband before going up?"

"Yes, but he didn't answer. I thought he might have the radio on, or maybe he was in the shower. The door was open, so I went in." She closed her eyes, her face drawn with pain as she recalled the horror.

Young as she was, she'd learned to keep herself under control, Dixon thought. It didn't mean she suffered less. On the contrary, often such persons suffered more because they repressed their feelings. He gave her a few moments.

"What phone did you use when you called 911?"

"I called from my room. I was so sick, I had to run, but I didn't make it." She turned the color of ashes and gulped as though she was going to throw up again. Again, Dixon waited till she had recovered.

"How long have you been married, Mrs. Trent?"

"Two years."

"Any children?"

"No. Douglas has a son by a previous marriage, Jonathan. He's married and has three children and lives in Toronto."

"Where do you keep your valuables?"

"We have a small wall safe in the den. It was broken into."

"What? You didn't mention this to the officers," he stated and asked for an explanation at the same time.

"No. I'm sorry. I forgot. Under the circumstances . . . I just forgot."

"Sure, I understand."

"We don't keep much in there anyway—a few hundred dollars for emergencies, that's all."

"Would you show me, please?"

The library was decorated in the same dark and heavy style as the living room; it seemed more oppressive because it was small, Dixon thought. The safe was set in the wall behind a Regency-style desk and covered by an oil painting of an English hunting scene. Typical, and the first place any thief would look. As had this one. The painting had been swung out and hung by the bottom hinge. An explosive charge, just enough to blow the safe open, had been inserted. There was no other damage. It was not necessarily the work of an expert, but it did suggest the perp at least had advance knowledge of what the job entailed. The explosion, rather than the breaking of glass in the kitchen door, was likely to have been what alerted Douglas Trent while he was unpacking, Dixon thought. At this stage, the distinction didn't appear to have any importance.

Dixon looked inside. "There's five hundred dollars here, but I don't see any jewelry."

"That would be upstairs in the bedroom."

"I'd like to take a look."

She led him back to the central hall and up the curving staircase to the second floor. At the landing she paused for a barely perceptible moment before turning to the right, away from the scene of the crime where detectives and technicians were still working. The room she entered was large, sumptuous, the walls paneled in rose damask and bathed in the glow of mauve silk-shaded lamps. There was no doubt this was the master suite; nevertheless, it didn't suit Emma Trent any more than the somber furnishings downstairs and next door. She indicated a white leather jewel box set on the bureau.

"Wait," he cautioned as she reached. "Is it locked?"

"No."

"Then, may I, please?"

Handling the lid at the corners in order not to smudge any latent prints, he raised it. Rings were in one tray, earrings in another, bracelets and necklaces in the lower sections. The gold had the rosy tone of eighteen carat. The stones, amethysts and aquamarines, though semiprecious, seemed to Ray Dixon to be of first quality. Their worth was greater than Emma Trent's casual manner had suggested. There was, in particular, a cabochon pearl ring circled by a triple row of rosecut diamonds that was very special. He couldn't imagine a thief leaving that behind. He stepped to one side.

"Anything missing?"

She looked quickly. "Nothing."

Nothing in the room had been touched. As far as Ray Dixon could tell, the perps hadn't even entered. Doc Fletcher agreed there had to have been more than one; three seemed excessive, so Dixon settled on two. Two seemed just right. They must have entered by way of the kitchen and headed for the den and the safe, Dixon thought. The sound of the explosion alerted Douglas Trent and he came out to investigate. They cut him off partway down the stairs. They started to hit him. He turned and ran back into the room, probably intending to lock the door against them, but they were too quick. They followed him inside and continued the attack.

Why? Why didn't they just run away? he wondered.

Was it because Douglas Trent could have identified them?

"We may need to be here a while longer, Mrs. Trent," Dixon told her. "But there's no need for you to stay up. In fact, there's no need for you to stay in the house. Is there someone you could spend the night with?"

For the first time in the interview Emma Trent looked directly at Sergeant Dixon. Then her glance shifted to the room down the hall. "You're not leaving him here overnight?"

"No, no, I'm sorry, you should have been informed. Mr. Trent has already been transported."

"Then I'll stay here. I can stay if I want, can't I? I can stay here in my own room."

"It's up to you, ma'am. Maybe you'd like to call somebody, a friend or relation, to stay with you?"

Who? she asked herself. She had no living relatives; she didn't count Jonathan, her stepson—they were anything but close and he lived in Canada. Emma Trent realized with a pang that, hard as she had worked to establish herself in the community, to be neighborly, she didn't have a single friend she could call on.

"No," she told Ray Dixon. "There's no one." She shook her head sadly.

Chapter ———————— THREE

Gwenn Ramadge watched the lights go on at the top floor of the East Village brownstone. She noted the time in her book: twelve-fifteen A.M. The threatened storm had bypassed the city. The night was calm, the air caressing. She prepared to wait.

Inside her new car, Gwenn Ramadge could stretch her legs, lean back against the leather upholstery, and enjoy her coffee and sandwich. Not dishwater coffee out of a plastic container, but her favorite brand of Colombian prepared at home and poured piping hot into a thermos. The sandwich also came from home—prosciutto and cheese on a wedge of crispy Italian bread. Business was good at Hart S and I, the small investigations agency Gwenn had inherited from its owner, and the car—a Volvo, used, but nevertheless a Volvo—was one of the first comforts to which she'd treated herself. Since a great deal of her work involved searching records and files, wheels were not strictly necessary. But when surveillance was required, the car provided not only transportation but shelter, too.

The client in this case was Laura Mancini, executive vice-president of Prestige Realty. As the name implied, the company handled high-priced real estate, both commercial and residential. The job—to check out one Bradford Keiser. This was not one of your standard employee background investigations. Mr. Keiser was not an employee of Prestige Realty. Ms. Mancini's interest was personal.

The first thing Gwenn discovered was that his real name was Humphrey Berg. The next, that he had a criminal record. The charges were dismaying: rape and sexual abuse. Laura Mancini had blanched when she heard and then chose to make excuses for him. She pointed out that though charged, he had never been convicted and he had never served time. Anyway, that was all in the past. Bradford, as she continued to call Berg, had set the past behind him, and she was willing to do the same. What she wanted was reassurance about his present status.

Gwenn had been tailing Berg for the past three weeks without observing anything worth reporting. However, being no amateur in the seduction of older women, he might expect that Ms. Mancini was having him watched and so he was behaving himself. How long would he continue? Gwenn could have hired another to take her place—just in case he'd made her—but Berg's antenna might pick him up, too. No, she decided to take a chance and leave him alone. She'd waited a week, which had brought her to this Wednesday night on which she knew Berg had a date with her client. Rather than tail the pair, watch him take Mancini home, and then follow him, Gwenn Ramadge decided to stake out his apartment. She was rewarded when he turned up after midnight in the company of an overweight but otherwise gorgeous redhead.

She got shots of them entering the brownstone together. Unfortunately, she couldn't get shots of their activities inside the apartment. She would get them coming out and that should be sufficient.

She had a hunch it was going to be a long night.

However, the redhead left earlier than anticipated. She came out alone and walked to the corner. The least Berg could have done was see her home, Gwenn thought. Or called her a cab. Was that being too old-fashioned? Meanwhile, the redhead had flagged a passing taxi. Evidently, she was perfectly capable of looking after herself.

Gwenn Ramadge turned on the ignition, and by the time the subject was in the taxi and the taxi was moving, she had pulled out and was following at a discreet distance. She kept the cab in sight till it pulled up in front of a small brick building in the Murray Hill section. Now she had an address. By observing which of the darkened windows lit up, she knew the subject lived on the sixth floor. In the morning, she would have the redhead's name.

Gwenn woke abruptly, knowing before she looked at the clock that she'd overslept. It was nine, which meant she'd had only five hours sleep, but she felt surprisingly rested. Gwenn stretched lazily, pleased with the previous night's work. It was, unfortunately, not the result Ms. Mancini had hoped for, but it was the truth and the truth was what she'd been contracted to discover. She called her office for messages and told her secretary, Marge, to contact Ms. Mancini and make an appointment for a meeting at her convenience. Then she prepared and ate a hearty breakfast.

Though Gwenn was what the fashion industry labeled "petite," she could afford to enjoy her food. Night classes twice a week at John Jay College and regular workouts at the gym kept her quick and agile in mind and body and burned up the calories.

Her hair was naturally blond, a dark honey in the winter but sun-streaked platinum in the summer. She wore it in a mop of short curls, which was both becoming and low maintenance. She could wash and towel it dry, run her fingers through it, and be ready to face the world, as she did that morning. She stepped into the shower, letting the warm water stream over the top of her head and onto her face, breasts, tummy, rounded hips, and down her well-shaped and strong legs. After lathering, she turned the faucet to Cool for the final rinse, then she stepped from the shower as fresh as if she'd had her regular eight hours of sleep.

She intended to identify Berg's girlfriend on her way to the office. There was no rush; it wasn't likely there was more than one tenant answering the description, certainly not one who also lived on the sixth floor. And it would be just as well if the subject wasn't around when Gwenn was asking her questions. She continued the morning's leisurely pace and studied what to wear, settling on a new outfit: a short charcoal linen skirt, rather than slacks, and a fitted daffodil yellow jacket. *Looks count*, Gwenn thought.

As a woman in a field dominated by men, Gwenn Ramadge regularly encountered discrimination, sometimes reverse discrimination. She saw no reason not to benefit from it, and she'd found that people were more inclined to cooperate when dealing with someone attractive. So she dressed to look her best, not flaunting her femininity, but not denying it either.

"I'm a private investigator," she told the superintendent when she arrived at the small, red-brick building in Murray Hill. "I'm tracing a lost heir. I have information that leads me to believe she lives here. Do you recognize this woman?" She handed him one of the Polaroids she'd taken the night before.

"That looks like Miss Rogers," he said cautiously.

"That's not the name I was given," Gwenn told him. "If she's the one, she's due to come into a lot of money. Would you take another look?"

The super took wire-rimmed glasses out of his shirt

pocket and scrutinized the photograph. "That's her. That's Theresa Rogers, for sure!"

People were also more inclined to help establish an identity when it meant good news rather than bad. Gwenn thanked the super, whose eyes now flashed with excitement, and returned to her car. Though the interview hadn't taken long, traffic was heavy, and when she got downtown, her regular parking lot was full. She lost more time till she found a space in one of the municipal fields on the far side of City Hall Park. Her office was across the street from the New York State Office Building on Broadway, a long walk back. She didn't mind. It was fun to saunter while everyone else around her was rushing. She enjoyed the chance to take time to admire the neo-classic court buildings, the stolid city and state complexes, the seats of government. She felt like a tourist and even bought herself a hot dog from a street vendor. But the good feeling didn't last past her office door. Marge Pratt jumped on her as soon as she walked in.

"I've been trying to get you! I called Howie's. They said you hadn't been in. I left a message anyway."

Howie's was a coffee shop where Gwenn often had breakfast when she didn't feel like cooking. "I ate at home."

"I called you at home. You weren't there," Marge complained. "I left a message on the machine."

"All right, Marge. What is it?"

"If you're not coming in, I wish you'd let me know. I've asked you to let me know where you can be reached."

That was not always possible and Gwenn was tired of explaining it. "I'm here now," she pointed out quietly.

"Ms. Mancini is coming in at one-thirty."

"Oh?"

"You said to make it at her convenience." A slow flush spread over Marge's sallow skin.

"I know."

"I could have given her a later appointment."

"It doesn't matter. I'm here now. Okay, Marge?"

"Yes, okay." She tried to smile, but her thin lips were stuck together. "I'm sorry," she managed to squeeze out.

"No. I should have told you where I would be. It's my fault. I'm sorry," Gwenn insisted. It always ended like this, she thought, suppressing her frustration. There had never been this kind of friction between her and Cordelia, she thought. She had done what she was told without argument. To be fair, Cordelia Hart had always made it a point to explain the case they were on and to keep Gwenn informed as to where she was, what she was doing, and why.

Gwenn Ramadge had come to work for Hart Security and Investigation not quite five years ago. It had taken her three years to earn her private investigator's license. She had been guided and encouraged by Cordelia Hart, the owner of the agency, who had inherited it from her father. Within months of Gwenn's getting her license, Cordelia Hart had a heart attack and died, leaving everything—the business and all her possessions, including a co-op on East Seventy-second Street—to Gwenn. Hart S and I specialized in corporate work: employee background checks, insurance scams, embezzlements. White-collar crime. There was a roster of regular clients. Business was adequate to maintain the one-woman office—no frills, no perks. Steady work. No dramas. No calls in the middle of the night. No shoot-outs. Then Anne Soffey, head of Soffey Cosmetics and an old client of Cordelia's, came to Gwenn for help. Her daughter had been drowned while on her honeymoon. The police were writing it off as an accident. Anne Soffey believed it was murder. She wanted Gwenn to prove it and to find the killer.

Gwenn took the case with great reluctance, but soon found herself caught up in the excitement of a homicide investigation. Two more brides were killed, and suddenly

Gwenn was treating the series of violent deaths like a puzzle, a game of wits. She felt challenged and enjoyed it. That frightened her. She solved the case, but she didn't like what it had done to her. *No more homicides*, she resolved. Never again. She returned to the placid, albeit boring, corporate work.

However, she had to admit that it was due largely to the Brides case and Anne Soffey's recommendations that business had improved so markedly. Mrs. Soffey sent Gwenn one corporate client after another, and each in turn sent others so that she was not only able to buy the Volvo, but to hire an office assistant, Marge Pratt. She had chosen Marge from a field of more qualified applicants, as Cordelia Hart had chosen her; Gwenn wanted to help someone as Cordelia had helped her.

Marge Pratt was twenty-seven, the same age Gwenn had been when she first came to Hart S and I. She was of medium height and build, with short, straight dark brown hair. Her eyes were a light gray. Nothing outstanding about her, no one feature to attract attention, and her manner didn't help. She was on the defensive whether the situation called for it or not. But when she smiled, there came a shy, tentative appeal from those gray eyes, changing her whole aspect. She had smiled during the interview and that was when Gwenn had decided to hire her. Unfortunately, she didn't smile often enough.

Marge Pratt's office skills were barely adequate, though better than Gwenn's had been when Cordelia took her on. But in the interview it had slipped out that Marge had been married less than a year and given birth only to have her husband walk out on her and the baby. She'd had the choice of going back home to the hills of West Virginia with her child and her shame, or sticking it out in the big city. That had struck a responsive chord in Gwenn. Though she'd never married, Gwenn had been enough in love to live with a man and become pregnant by him. That man, a well-known photographer, had also backed off. Gwenn had chosen to have her child, stay, and make it on her own. Cordelia Hart had hired Gwenn in spite of her condition; Gwenn had hired Marge because of it. Gwenn had had a miscarriage and lost her baby. Marge had carried to term and delivered a son, determined to raise him on her own.

Marge Pratt had had several jobs before coming to work for Gwenn. She had no trouble getting them, but couldn't seem to keep them. She was willing; she worked hard. Maybe that was the problem, Gwenn thought, maybe she was trying too hard. Could be that she realized the long list of jobs in a short span didn't speak well. Gwenn would have liked to tell her to relax, that she had no intention of firing her, but she sensed Marge might have felt she was being pitied. Better leave things as they were, she decided, at the same time promising herself to put Marge more into the picture.

"Anything else?"

"No."

"Okay, then." She checked the clock over Marge's head: ten minutes after one. "Send Ms. Mancini in as soon as she gets here."

Gwenn went into her office. It wasn't much larger than the anteroom, but it did have a window with a view of City Hall. Aside from the good quality broadloom in a bright blue tweed that covered the suite, both rooms were furnished with an eye to practicality. Each had a metal desk, a row of filing cabinets, and a small, free-standing utility closet. In Gwenn's office the only concession to her position was a pair of chairs for clients. Gwenn settled herself, pulled out the notes on last night's surveillance, reviewing and organizing at the same time. She would have liked to have a written report ready for the client, but there was no time to dictate it, much less to have it typed—Marge's typing was excruciatingly slow, though accurate. A later appointment would certainly have been better, Gwenn acknowledged; she should have informed Marge she wouldn't be coming straight in from home. A light tap at the door interrupted her thoughts. Already? The client was not only punctual, she was early. Most of the women who came to her in these situations were restless and anxious. Laura Mancini was not the only one.

Gwenn Ramadge had made it known to Anne Soffey and to all present and prospective clients that she would take only corporate work. Then, about four months after the Brides case was cleared, a woman walked in and asked her to do a premarital checkup—on her boyfriend. The woman was nearing forty; she was attractive in an elegant, hard-edged way. She wanted Gwenn to investigate the man she was on the verge of moving in with. She wanted to be sure he was what he represented himself to be. She wanted to know his marital status, health, and sexual orientation—though not necessarily in that order.

In the past, a father might initiate such an investigation to save his daughter from a fortune hunter. The girl would have been too besotted to think of it. But these were not girls who came to Gwenn; they were women, and they were not without experience. In fact, in most instances they'd been stung once before. Most were at least in their mid-thirties; all were upwardly mobile, ambitious, determined: workaholics. They were close to the top of the corporate ladder, but they lacked one asset—a man of their own. Thus they considered themselves incomplete, personally and professionally. They were unable to fill in the column on the resumé headed: *Married, Children.* Some had a "relationship," but it wasn't enough. They wanted a formal commitment. Without it, their success was tarnished.

Through her investigation, Gwenn was able to save a

number of these women from disappointment and heart-break. At the very least, she was able to save them considerable embarrassment. Her reputation spread through what was becoming known as *the old girl network.*

Laura Mancini strode directly to Gwenn's desk and took her usual chair at the right. She held herself rigid, hands clasped in her lap. Her makeup was perfect, every hair in place. Gwenn knew that inside she was shaking.

"It's not good news. I'm sorry," she told Laura Mancini.

Some of the tension seeped out of the woman, though not all.

Gwenn laid out the Polaroids she'd taken the night before in front of Berg's house, one by one and in sequence, the time marked in the lower right hand corner of each. "As you see, she was there for a little over two hours."

"There could be an innocent explanation."

Gwenn didn't comment.

"Do you know who the woman is?"

"I have her name and address. I can give it to you, or I can speak to her, if you'd like."

Laura Mancini considered. "No. It's not necessary. I'll talk to Bradford."

Gwenn kept her face expressionless. It wasn't up to her what clients did with the information she made available.

"You'll send a written report with your bill, please. To my home, of course, not the office."

"Of course."

"I don't suppose there's any point in continuing the surveillance?"

"It would be a waste of my time and your money." She said it gently.

Mancini sighed and got to her feet.

"Ms. Mancini," Gwenn called to her. She gathered

the photographs into an envelope and held it out. "These are yours."

"Oh, yes." She took it and stuffed it into her luxurious lizard handbag. Then she turned and walked out. Without shaking hands. Without saying thank you. They seldom said thank you when the answer wasn't the one they wanted, Gwenn thought. Sometimes, they said it later.

Chapter
FOUR

By the time the police left and Emma Trent could finally retire, it was close to four A.M. She closed her bedroom door firmly behind her and, after a moment's hesitation, locked it and leaned her back against it. It wasn't till then that the full horror of what had happened that night hit her. The hard knot of shock that had insulated her and protected her from the time she discovered Douglas, through her call to the police, their arrival and interrogation, melted at last and she began to cry—softly at first, then in increasing intensity. Douglas was dead. She threw herself on the bed, sobs wracking her body. Douglas was dead.

It took a long time to cry herself out, but gradually the sobs subsided and she drifted into an exhausted, heavy sleep.

The morning light probed at her eyelids, but for a long time she resisted opening her eyes. She wasn't ready to wake up. As she lay there trying to shut out the world, she heard the back doorbell. Reluctantly, she rolled over to look at the bedside clock: seven-thirty. Who could it be so early? The police?

The doorbell rang again.

She sat up, swung her legs over the side, and walked

over to the mirror. Her face was puffy, her eyes reddened. She had slept in her clothes and they looked it.

The bell rang for the third time.

Peering out the window, Emma saw her neighbor from across the street standing at the kitchen door. She ran a comb through her hair and then went down to let her in.

"Emma!" Sue Wanamaker exclaimed. "I just heard. I was baby-sitting the grandchildren and I just got home. What a terrible thing! Poor Douglas! I can't believe it. Have the police any idea who did it?"

Emma shook her head.

Sue Wanamaker gushed on. "According to the radio, it was a botched burglary—nothing was taken," she added, scrutinizing Emma.

"The police think Douglas interrupted them."

"Ah..." the neighbor nodded sagely. "That makes sense. We're not safe in our own houses anymore. Are you all right? That's a stupid question. Of course you aren't. How could you be? I came over to help. Now you just tell me what you want me to do," she said, and clucked and pushed her way past Emma and into the kitchen.

"Thank you, but there's nothing."

"Now, now, of course there is. First of all we've got to get this door fixed."

Mrs. Wanamaker was a thin, gaunt but big-boned woman accustomed to taking charge. As head of an amateur drama group, she had a tendency to dramatize events. Here was a situation that would give full scope to both talents. She stood in the center of the big, family-style kitchen as she might on center stage. "There's a lot to do. More than you realize. But not to worry. I'll take care of everything. So, before we start—have you had breakfast?" She was bossy, but also kind.

"I was just going to put on the coffee."

"That's not breakfast. How about eggs and toast?"

Emma shook her head. "I couldn't."

But she was touched. She'd always considered Sue Wanamaker a busybody. Plus which she knew the woman had been close to Douglas's first wife, so she'd resisted her neighborly overtures. She wanted to show her appreciation now, but Emma Trent was by nature a very private person and she didn't feel up to having Sue Wanamaker, no matter how well-meaning, underfoot.

"It's very kind of you, but I can manage."

Sue Wanamaker went ahead as though she hadn't spoken. "Then there's the school. You'll be calling off classes, naturally. It wouldn't be seemly to conduct them. And you're not up to it anyway."

That hadn't occurred to Emma. There were classes scheduled and, of course, she'd have to cancel. She hadn't given a thought to anything but the horror with which she was locked up inside this house. "I'll have to call . . ."

"No need," her efficient neighbor assured her. "I'll just run over to the studio and put up a sign for you: *Closed till further notice.* Oh, and if you'll give me your keys, I'll go in and put a message on your answering machine. That'll take care of the calls that come in. There'll be plenty."

"Yes, that would be good. I hadn't thought of it. Thanks, Sue."

"They'll be calling here, too, starting any minute," she warned. "Let them go through the machine, too. You don't have to pick up unless you feel like it. I wouldn't suggest taking the phone off the hook."

"Oh, no."

"Is there anyone who should be notified? Anyone in Douglas's family? His son? Have you called Jonathan?"

My God, Jonathan! How could she have forgotten him? The school and whatever other details Sue Wanamaker might come up with were one thing, but Jonathan . . . She should have called him last night. The shock of discovering Douglas had blotted out all other considerations. She shook her head.

"Not yet."

"You should do it first thing. And it's not too soon to think about the funeral arrangements." Sue Wanamaker's gaunt face softened. "Did the police say anything about when they might release . . . the body?"

But Emma wasn't listening. How was she going to tell Jonathan about his father's death?

In response to his stepmother's call, Jonathan Trent took the next available flight out of Toronto and arrived, bag and baggage, that Thursday evening. Emma met him at the front door.

"I'm sorry," she said. She didn't offer a hug or a kiss. They never touched each other, these two.

"Are you?" He stared at her.

She met his look. "Yes, I am."

Jonathan Trent was actually three years older than his stepmother, but the extra pounds he carried, along with his wire-rimmed glasses and receding hairline, made him look older. He shrugged, then signaled the driver to bring in his luggage.

She was dismayed at the amount. "How long do you plan to stay?"

"Depends."

She didn't ask on what. Emma had long since resigned herself to Jonathan's resentment of her. At the beginning, she had tried very hard to make him like her. She had tried to convince him that she truly loved his father. She tried to reach him through Sheila, his wife, taking her to lunch and on shopping trips. She'd fussed over his children—giving them presents, spoiling them. She'd even gone so far as to side with Jonathan in the frequent arguments between father and son. It united them by turning their anger from each other against her.

Jonathan shot her a look of cool dislike and, leaving the luggage piled in the hall where the driver had set it, strode into the living room. She trailed behind.

"I want to hear exactly what happened."

He made her go through it all from the time she approached the house and noticed the lights upstairs, what she saw and what she did upon discovery of the murder, till the police arrived and took charge. He didn't spare her.

She didn't spare herself.

"Do the police have any idea who did it?" Jonathan asked.

"No. They wanted to know if anything had been taken."

"Was anything missing?"

"The safe was blown open."

"That's not what I asked you."

"As far as I can tell, nothing is missing."

Jonathan carried his bags up to the third floor, taking the room that had been his since he was a boy. He didn't suggest going out for dinner, but he did accept the light meal Emma prepared for the two of them. Conversation was down to a minimum. Afterwards, he settled himself in the library to review his father's papers. Emma retired early.

To that point, Jonathan Trent had not offered one word of sympathy, nor any expression of condolence to his father's widow.

Jeremiah Bates closed the store promptly at midnight and started for home. He took a shortcut through the heavily wooded, park-like section between the Maple Grove Cemetery and the Van Wyck Expressway. In the daytime, when the weather was good, people brought blankets and did their sunbathing there. Though there was no history of gangs or druggies hanging out, people avoided the area at night. He wouldn't have been there himself, but his car was in the garage with transmission problems and he couldn't afford a rental. Anyway, he wasn't afraid. It was a nice night and he didn't mind the walk.

Bates was the night manager of the new Waldbaum's. It was a good job, but the hours were bad. He had little time to spend with his family—his wife, Sylvia, and the two girls, three-year-old Greta and Anna, age five. There was no time at all for his great passion: the Opera Society. It was a semiprofessional group, but immensely prestigious. Jerry, as he preferred to be called, was a short, rotund man with crimped blond hair and a sweet, true tenor. Two years before he had sung the role of Don José in *Carmen*. It was the high point of his life. Since getting the night job he'd had to forgo the chance to appear in *Turandot* because rehearsals were at night. He had been promised a day job, but they kept putting him off. Finally, he was told that if he insisted on shifting to day work, he would have to take a demotion and a cut in pay. Making ends meet on his present salary was tough enough. He couldn't ask Sylvia to do with less, he thought, and picked up his pace.

As he did so, he suddenly became aware of a flicker of light up ahead among the trees. It went out almost immediately. After a moment or two it reappeared, sputtered, and went out again. Someone trying to light a cigarette? If so, he'd better be careful, Bates thought. It had been a dry spring and over in New Jersey and out on the Island they'd already had brush fires. Warnings were being issued. The next Bates knew there was a small explosion and a bonfire appeared to have been lit. Yellow and blue flames, denoting some sort of starter fluid had been used, licked into the darkness and made a circle of light. A dark figure crouched over the fire.

"Hey, you! Kid! What are you doing? What's going on?"

Slowly, the figure turned toward Bates, but with the firelight behind him, his face was in shadow. The two of them remained like that for several seconds, neither moving. Then suddenly, the figure straightened out of his crouch and ran.

"Hey, you! Come back!"

Bates's instinct was to give chase, but the fire had taken hold and was growing fast. It was throwing off sparks that ignited new fires among the dead, dry underbrush. Taking off his jacket, Jerry Bates began to beat at the flames. He was making it worse. Choking on the smoke, he turned away to find a telephone and call for help.

The way it looked to Ray Dixon, the case was open and shut. Forensics had taken blood samples, dusted for prints, looked for threads of clothing, hair, skin scrapings. Routine. Ray expected no surprises. Late in the afternoon he had gotten Doc Fletcher to confirm that the death blows had been administered by heavy wooden slabs or bats. The previous night's search of the house and grounds had been unproductive; so had a subsequent search of the streets and neighboring gardens. Dixon couldn't see the perps walking around carrying the bats. So what had they done with them? He decided not to speculate.

Having completed his report, Ray turned it in and went home for some sleep.

He wasn't due back on duty till four P.M. Friday. As far as he could tell, there was no need for him to go in any sooner. If anything should turn up, he'd hear about it.

When he arrived, there was a stack of messages on his desk, all from the same person—Jonathan Trent. He checked his book; yes, that was Douglas Trent's son by his first wife. Before he had sorted through the rest of his messages, a man entered the squad room and headed straight to him. Dixon could tell he had a very big chip on his shoulder.

"I've been trying to get hold of you since morning."

"You are . . . ?"

"Jonathan Trent."

"Of course. I've just come on duty, Mr. Trent."

"I would think that under the circumstances . . ." he broke off with a lugubrious sigh. "I suppose one case is pretty much like another to you."

"That's where you're wrong, Mr. Trent. Each and every victim receives the same attention. We expend the same effort to discover and apprehend the guilty party. If that's what you mean. You could have spoken to my partner."

Trent flushed. "Let's not argue. I'm not here to blame you or anybody else."

Dixon nodded and motioned him to the chair beside his desk. "What can I do for you, sir?"

Still scowling, Trent took the seat. He did not make an impressive appearance, Dixon thought. He was fat and balding. So far, he had behaved like a spoiled child. Douglas Trent, despite the terrible battering, had struck Dixon as dignified. The son didn't take after the father.

"I demand a thorough investigation of my father's murder."

"You'll get it."

"When?"

"The investigation has begun, Mr. Trent."

"I can't see that you're doing anything. You didn't even contact me."

"We spoke to your stepmother, Mrs. Emma Trent,

immediately upon the report of your father's death. She did call you?"

"Yes, and I took the first available flight. Got in yesterday evening."

"Just what is the problem, Mr. Trent?"

"I went straight to the house. I expected the police would be there."

"We were there Wednesday night and into Thursday morning. The crime-scene detectives took photographs, dusted for prints, collected blood samples. When they finished, they left."

"What about my father's wife? Shouldn't you have brought her in for questioning?"

"As I said, I spoke to Mrs. Trent right after she called 911 to report the crime." He paused to allow the son to comment or to indicate more specifically what he was after, though the way he had referred to his stepmother was a pretty good indication. "The assault took place sometime between nine P.M. and one A.M. Mrs. Trent conducted a class at her studio, which lasted till after nine. She showered, changed, and caught the last showing of the feature at the movie house around the corner. The ticket seller knows her and remembers her buying a ticket, because the last show had already started. Several persons who know her saw her in the crowd when the show let out at eleven forty-five."

"How about during the show? Did someone sit with her? Can anyone vouch she didn't leave the theater? I don't know if you're familiar with the area, Sergeant, but it's only a short walk from the movie theater to my father's house."

"I realize Mrs. Trent could have slipped out of the theater without being seen; there are several side exits. She could have walked to the house, did what had to be done, and returned," Dixon said. "But fit as she is, I don't think she has the physical capacity to overcome your father. I believe, as does the medical examiner, that it took at least two people to inflict the injuries your father sustained." Dixon hesitated. As a rule, he avoided offering painful details to the family of the victim, but sometimes it was unavoidable. "I'm afraid the wake will have to be held with a closed casket."

Jonathan Trent grew pale. He swallowed a couple of times and remained silent for so long that Dixon thought he had given up.

"She could have hired someone."

Dixon hadn't expected an outright accusation. "Are you telling me that your father and his second wife weren't getting along? That the marriage was in trouble?"

"That's right."

"Are you accusing your stepmother of having your father killed?"

"I'm pointing out the possibility." He was sweating heavily.

"I see. Anybody else know they weren't getting along?"

Trent shrugged. He produced a pack of cigarettes and lit one.

"How do you know?" Dixon asked.

"I was present when they argued. Violently, sometimes."

"What about?"

"Her behavior, mostly."

"What about it? Come on, Mr. Trent. These are serious allegations. You've opened a can of worms. You're going to have to be more explicit."

"She had lovers."

Dixon remained impassive. "You're going to have to be more specific, sir."

"I don't have names, addresses, and telephone numbers!" he flared.

"Don't worry, Mr. Trent. If what you say is true, we'll get them."

"It's true, all right." He puffed nervously.

Dixon watched. "How did you and your father get along?"

"Me and my dad? We got along just fine."

"You worked for him."

"I'm in charge of the Canadian office."

"There were no differences about policy or your conduct of the business?"

"There were differences, naturally, but we resolved them."

"This particular business trip your father took—what was the reason for it?"

"No reason. It was routine. He came up regularly."

"And he found everything in order?"

"Come on, Sergeant! Emma called me at eight yesterday morning in my home in Oshawa. That's about thirty miles outside Toronto. I was there. I hadn't just walked in the door when the phone rang. I was in my bed, sleeping. You can ask my wife, for God's sake!" he sputtered in indignation.

"Your father wasn't due back here till Thursday. He came a day early. Any idea why?"

"None. We were finished. Everything was in order and he went on to Vancouver. We were negotiating to buy some land. He was supposed to return by way of Toronto and spend another night at my home. I have three children. He's crazy about them. Instead, he called to say he was going straight to New York. He didn't say why and I didn't ask."

"Who else did he notify?"

"His office, I suppose."

"Not his wife?"

The son was silent for a moment. "How do you know he didn't call her? Just because she says so?"

He had a point, Dixon thought. "We'll look into it," he promised. "Thank you for coming in. Where can we reach you if we should need you? Are you going back to Toronto?"

"Not right away. There's a lot of business to take care of."

"And the will," Dixon added. "So you'll be staying . . . ?"

"At the house." Trent was surprised by the question.

"With your stepmother?"

"It's my father's house. I have every right to be there, at least till the will is read. Afterwards, well, my dear stepmother may be in for a surprise."

"What kind of surprise, Mr. Trent? If you have information that's pertinent to the investigation, please tell me straight out."

"My father intended to change his will."

"Intended?"

"He mentioned it."

"To whom?" The man couldn't make a flat-out statement, Dixon thought. "To you? How about to his wife? Did he tell her?"

Jonathan Trent took one last drag and ground out the cigarette in the ash tray Dixon pushed toward him. His eyes glittered behind the tinted lenses. "I don't know," he admitted, and the eagerness was gone.

"Is there anything else you'd like to . . . suggest?" Dixon asked.

"I'll be honest with you, Sergeant. My wife and I disapproved of the marriage from the beginning. To start with, there was the age difference. She's younger than me, for God's sake! My father was rich, not in the class of the Rockefellers or Kennedys, but he had more money than she'd ever got close to. Her background was murky. She never talked about her family or friends. She was a chorus girl. She'd been in a couple of road companies of

Broadway shows, that's all. We were convinced she was marrying my father for his money. We insisted he hire a detective to investigate her." He took a deep breath and exhaled. "She came out poor but honest." He was heavy on the sarcasm. "None of us ever saw the actual report, of course."

"You think your father was hiding something?"

"He had a prenuptial agreement drawn up; I don't think he would have done that if he didn't have some doubts." Having made his point finally, Trent got up. "I'll be hearing from you, Sergeant Dixon." It was not a question.

Dixon nodded. "One thing, Mr. Trent. Do you know the name of the agency your father hired?"

"Hart Security and Investigations."

Dixon had never heard of it. He looked it up in the Yellow Pages. It was there, just a single line listing. That meant one of two things: they couldn't afford an ad, or they had as much business as they could handle. In due course he'd find out which. Tomorrow was Saturday, one of the few Saturdays he got off. The Mets were in town, and he had a ticket.

It could wait till Monday.

Chapter_____
_____ FIVE

On Saturday, Gwenn Ramadge went to the beach with Lew Sackler. Despite using a Number 30 sunblock, she got a bad burn and was still flaming red on Monday. It was worth it. Gwenn loved the sea and was a strong swimmer. Besides, it was getting to be more and more fun to be with Lew.

Gwenn first met Detective First Grade Lew Sackler on the Brides case. He was thirty and very good looking. He had a broad, open face with a high brow, and dark hair that swept back from a widow's peak. There had been a mutual attraction from the start, but nothing passionately compelling. They liked each other. They were comfortable together. After the Brides case was cleared, they went on three or four dates. Though they had similar interests, there wasn't any spark. By unspoken agreement, the relationship was allowed to cool—before it had ever gotten hot.

Then about a month ago, Lew Sackler called again. Lew and Gwenn had an early dinner, got caught up on their respective careers, and then went to a movie. He didn't put any moves on her, but he did call again the very next morning. They began to see each other regularly, and began talking about their childhoods and their families. Lew told her about growing up on Flatbush

Avenue. His father was a cop, known and respected by everybody on his beat. Lew's ambition had been to be just like his father, but police work was different now. The patrol cop was confined to his car, with no real contact between him and the people it was his job to protect. The current Police Commissioner was trying to restore the concept of "the beat cop," but it was Lew's opinion that times had changed and it was impossible to bring back the past. He told her how proud he was that he'd made detective. He shared his worry over his father, who was a diabetic and who, since his mother's death, had relocated to Miami Beach.

Gwenn had grown up in Manhattan, an only child too, but under very different circumstances. She lived in a seven-room apartment on Fifth Avenue overlooking Central Park. She attended a prestigious private school, the Cummings School for Girls. Every day after classes, the live-in maid, Helene, took Gwenn to the park for skating or bicycling. On Saturdays, it was the Children's Concert at Carnegie Hall. On Sundays, the museums and galleries. She was taught to consider attendance not as an obligation, but as a privilege. She graduated Barnard College.

The day after her graduation, her father announced he was bankrupt. Somehow, Oscar Ramadge had contrived to hang on until she was through school. He couldn't have lasted a day longer.

The apartment and everything in it had to go. Paula Ramadge sold her jewelry, even the oriental rugs and fine silver hollowware that had been part of her dowry. With the proceeds they were able to relocate to Cuernavaca, Mexico, the "in" place for expatriate Americans. Gwenn stayed behind and faced the reality of earning a living. She met Ray Eagen, a top fashion photographer, and learned that passion was no guarantee of character. As soon as Ray learned Gwenn was pregnant, he dumped her. Then she met Cordelia Hart, who saw her through the physical and emotional trauma of the miscarriage. Cordelia taught her that there were good and decent people in the world. Gwenn was beginning to believe Sackler might be one of them.

They continued to see each other, to feel each other out. Lew still didn't make a pass, and Gwenn felt she was being seriously and respectfully courted. She liked it. She wasn't sure how she would respond when the time came, but for now, it was nice.

Naturally, Lew's free time depended on his case load. She could more easily adjust her work schedule than he could. Having spent most of the weekend with him, Gwenn was, on this Monday morning, faced with a backlog of reports to write up. She'd come to the office early and was so immersed she didn't hear the tap at the door. Finally, Marge Pratt poked her head in.

"There's a police officer to see you."

Gwenn's green eyes lit up. She felt a surge of pleasure. Lew! Then she thought, no. Marge knew Lew. She would have said his name if that's who it was.

"Ask him to come in."

"Sergeant Ray Dixon." Ray introduced himself and held out his open shield case for her to get a good look at his ID. Gwenn noted he was from Queens Homicide.

She waved him to a chair. "What can I do for you, Sergeant Dixon?"

"I understand you own the Hart Agency," he said with his usual, quiet deference.

"That's right. I inherited it from Cordelia Hart. Her father was the original founder."

"I'm interested in an investigation conducted by the agency a little over two years ago. You were hired to look into the background of a certain Emma Bliss."

Gwenn frowned. "It doesn't ring a bell. I was relatively

new at the time. I didn't conduct investigations. Mostly, I did library research."

"I assume Miss Hart did the job herself, then. There must be records," Dixon suggested.

"You can see our space is limited." Gwenn indicated both her office and the tiny reception area. "When I took over I had to get rid of a lot of stuff. If what you're talking about was an employee check, then I might have a file on the particular company and I could find it that way."

"This was a personal background search."

"Ah . . . I'm sorry."

"Miss Hart never spoke of the case?"

"I don't recall that she did."

Dixon hadn't intended to reveal his reason for seeking the information, but Gwenn Ramadge impressed him as honest and he had no other line to pursue. "The client was Douglas Trent."

She still showed no reaction.

"Don't you read the papers, Miss Ramadge?" He had expected to impress her.

"Apparently not as closely as I should. What did I miss?"

The moment of irritation passed. "Douglas Trent was attacked and killed in his home this past Wednesday night. Emma Bliss was his wife. She found him."

Gwenn frowned. "I did see that, yes, but I didn't pay attention to names. According to the papers, it was an attempted burglary. These things happen so frequently that—though I hate to say it—I've begun to take them in stride. I've lost sensitivity."

"We all have." Nice woman, Dixon thought.

Understanding, for a cop, Gwenn thought. "As I recall, the victim had been away on a business trip and wasn't due back till the following day. His wife wasn't expecting him and was at the movies. Isn't that right?"

"You attach particular significance to that? Why?"

"I wondered if the perps knew he wasn't supposed to be home? Would they have gone into the house unless they were certain it was empty?"

"But there was somebody home."

"Bad luck," Gwenn replied. "For Mr. Trent."

He stared at her. "Anything else, Miss Ramadge?"

Her sunburned face grew even redder. "No. Even if I'd read the story with full attention, the names wouldn't have been familiar. As I told you, if Miss Hart did conduct an investigation for Douglas Trent into his wife's past, I knew nothing about it."

"You could search the records. I'd appreciate that."

"I assume that you're carrying the case and that you have reason to question the wife's alibi."

"Now, Miss Ramadge..."

"How did you find out Douglas Trent hired the Hart Agency?"

"Again, Miss Ramadge, you know better than to ask," he chided, but a smile hovered at the corners of his mouth.

"And, of course, you know better than to answer," she retorted.

At home that evening Gwenn acknowledged she had been less than strictly honest with Sergeant Dixon. Confidentiality was the first thing Cordelia Hart had impressed on her protégé. Loyalty to the client was a part of her code of conduct. It was the private investigator's responsibility to look long and hard at the situation and the evidence before deviating. She didn't know anything about the Trent case. Though it was true Cordelia had not mentioned it, she had let Dixon think the file was no longer in existence. Actually, she wasn't sure. When she took over the business, Gwenn had not cleaned house indiscriminately. She had not chosen a date arbitrarily

and then destroyed all files prior to it. What she had done
was take the documents home with her and at leisure
had transferred them to the computer. She was still in
the process. Chances were good that the file along with
the report Cordelia had turned in to Douglas Trent was
in one of the bundles in the closet of the spare room.
Cordelia had kept impeccable records. Unfortunately,
the temp Gwenn had hired to help move them hadn't
paid attention to sequence. It took a while for Gwenn,
sitting cross-legged on the floor, to sort through, sometimes having to examine page by page, but she finally
found what she was looking for. Cordelia had never
thrown anything away: that was another of her precepts.
The report was short; it consisted of only three pages,
yet as Gwenn carried it over to her desk for study, she
found that she was very excited.

The first thing Cordelia had discovered about the subject was that Emma Bliss was not her real name. She
was born Emma Brodsky. She'd changed it for theatrical
purposes. Fair enough, Gwenn thought.

A plain name, but not a plain girl, not if you judged
by the eight-by-ten glossies Cordelia had included. Admittedly, they were professional shots calculated to bring
out the best in the subject, heightened by good lighting
and the expert application of makeup. Nevertheless, there
was a very special quality about this girl. Her face was
a perfect oval, skin clear; eyes serene; light brown hair,
long, straight, and silky. She was the girl next door, everybody's sweetheart. What lay under that demure exterior?
What had Cordelia found?

Emma Brodsky was born in Chicago, of Polish parents.
They operated a small laundry. They were very religious,
and Emma, their only child, was strictly raised. Early on
she showed an interest in the dance, and it was evident
she had natural talent. The parents were proud, but they
didn't have the money to give her the training she needed

to be accepted by a top ballet company. At fifteen, when other teenagers worked during the summer in the local supermarket or five-and-dime, or baby-sat, Emma Brodsky danced in the line in nightclubs and discos. She brought home good money.

By the time she was seventeen, her parents had saved enough to fulfill their dream of a return visit to their hometown of Cracow. The cheapest ticket was via the national airline. The plane crashed.

Emma's only remaining family was in Poland. She had never seen them. She didn't speak the language. She thought she would be more lonely there with them than she was here by herself. At that time she was working in a ballroom dance studio. One of the men she partnered in local competitions asked her to marry him. Conrad Hailey seemed both honest and realistic. He was sixty-six and he had a heart condition, he told her. He didn't expect to live much longer; another five years at most, according to his doctor. In return for spending those years with him, Emma would inherit—not a fortune—but a comfortable sum of money. Used to living from hand to mouth, the arrangement appealed to her. Even more appealing was the prospect of not being alone anymore.

Conrad Hailey kept part of his promise. He died within two years. According to the autopsy, he died because he hadn't taken his medication.

Hailey's family blamed the young wife. She hadn't given it to him. She hadn't taken proper care of him. She'd left him alone. She'd been out of the house at one of her dance classes when he had the attack. She was a young woman married to a man on the edge of senility. She wanted his money. But they couldn't prove intent. They couldn't even prove negligence.

In a penciled aside on the original worksheet, but not included in the official report, Cordelia Hart suggested: *A case can be made for Hailey's having deceived his young bride.*

He misrepresented his financial situation. There was, in actuality, very little money to begin with, and this he spent freely in his last years, without regard for what would be left for Emma. Knowing the end was near and the money just about gone, he could simply have stopped taking the medication and let himself die.

The report continued:

Emma went back to her nightclub and ballroom work, but the rumors and the whispers and the innuendoes followed her. She changed her name to Emma Bliss and moved to New York.

Douglas Trent met her at a disco where he was entertaining clients. He was immediately attracted. He had recently lost his wife of twenty years and after a brief courtship, he asked Emma to marry him.

At the time, Trent was forty-six. She had just passed twenty-one, but the age difference was much less than in her first marriage. Also, Douglas Trent was a vigorous, sexually active man. The only obstacle was Trent's son. It was largely to pacify him that Trent had hired Hart S and I.

Cordelia interviewed people who had known Emma when she was Mrs. Hailey. According to them, she'd been more nurse than wife. She had certainly fulfilled her part of the bargain. There was no boyfriend on the side. If there was, she'd done a good job of hiding him. Nor was there any indication of subsequent illicit relationships.

In another penciled aside, Cordelia pointed out: *Though Emma worked in what might be considered a corrupt atmosphere, her behavior was moral. Some of the dancers at the disco dated customers and were encouraged to do so. Emma Bliss appears to have passed through untouched.*

Gwenn sat back, tilted her head to stretch the tight muscles in her neck. Whoever had informed Sergeant Dixon about Trent's investigation of his intended bride would be disappointed. There was nothing pejorative in

it. In her private asides, Cordelia Hart had expressed
faith in the young woman. No need to withold the report,
Gwenn thought. She would make a copy and pass it on
to Sergeant Dixon without reservations. She dialed the
number he had given her.

The phone rang several times. According to the hours
he'd noted on the card, he should still be on duty. So,
he was out. There was no urgency. She was on the point
of hanging up.

"Homicide. Detective Sackler."

She was surprised. "Lew! It's me, Gwenn."

So was he. "Hi. How are you?"

"Fine."

There was a pause, uncertainty at both ends. "You've
got the wrong line," he told her. "This is Sergeant Dixon's extension."

"I know. That's who I'm calling."

"You are?"

"It's about the Trent case. He came to see me this
morning."

"He came to see you about the Trent case?"

"That's right. I found the information he wanted. I
can send it over or he can pick it up tomorrow. Whatever's most convenient."

"What've you got? Can you tell me about it?"

"Why not? Sure. It seems that before he married the
current Mrs. Trent, Douglas Trent hired Cordelia to
investigate her past."

"Your Cordelia?"

"Right. Trent's son and his wife were convinced she
was marrying him for his money. Sergeant Dixon wanted
to know the results of the investigation. I wasn't sure I
still had the file."

"But you did?"

"Yes."

"And?"

"There's a story. Emma Trent was married once before to an older man and he died. His family said it was her fault, that she was negligent."

"Was she?"

"Not so they could prove it. According to Cordelia, Emma Bliss Trent was honest and up front about the whole thing."

"So now you're ready to turn over the material. Oh, Ms. Ramadge, you are wonderful."

"What's that supposed to mean?"

"If the report had been pejorative, would you be offering to turn it over?"

"Douglas Trent was our client. It's my obligation to make sure there was nothing detrimental to him in the report."

"He's dead!"

"Nevertheless... And I don't appreciate your suggestion that I would withhold evidence."

"I never said that."

"You implied it." Indignation rang in her voice. "If there was anything in that report with a bearing on the current investigation, I would have done exactly as I'm doing now. You couldn't expect me to turn the file over without examining it first."

"No, of course not. Relax, Gwenn. I'm not trying to tell you how to run your business. I know better."

"I'm glad to hear it."

They both started to laugh.

"Anyway, there's a new development," Lew told her. "The baseball bats used to beat up Trent have been found. Somebody tried to burn them."

"What?"

"You know that woody area near the Queens courthouse and Van Wyck? Thursday night, the night manager of the new Waldbaum's was walking home from work when he spotted a kid starting a bonfire. He yelled and the kid ran. He didn't chase him because he was more concerned with putting out the fire. But it had already taken hold, so he called the fire department. They put it out without any trouble and found the bats barely charred. They turned them over to us."

"This is Monday, four days later," Gwenn pointed out.

"Right. The way things stand between the departments, that's pretty quick communication."

She smiled to herself, but was quickly serious again. "There's no doubt they're the murder weapons?"

"Every test has been positive. The lab has yet to do a DNA test. If they don't get a match with Douglas Trent, I'll take you to dinner at the Rainbow Room."

"Did the perps leave any traces?"

"One thing at a time, Ms. Ramadge. Patience. Things are developing. We had a call from one of the Trents' neighbors. She noticed a kid hanging around the house a few days before the break-in."

"Who?"

"Local teenager with a shady reputation."

"So?"

"So Dixon's over there now talking to him."

"Is Dixon new? I haven't heard you mention him."

"He's been on the sergeant's list waiting assignment for months. We had an opening and he got it."

"So are the two of you working together?"

"Right. How about I come over tomorrow night and pick up the report? Then we can have dinner."

"At the Rainbow Room?"

"I wish. How about the new Chinese place on Second?"

"If that's the best you can do." She started to hang up.

"Gwenn! We're keeping it quiet about the bats, for the time being. Okay?"

"Got it."

But Lew called the next morning before Gwenn left the house.

"Would it be all right if I came by to pick up that report now?"

"Sure. When?"

"Half an hour?"

"Fine."

"And about tonight . . . I have to cancel."

"Oh. I'm sorry."

She waited, but he didn't explain.

Chapter

SIX

Emma Trent decided it was time to pick up the pieces of her life. Jonathan had settled in. He'd consulted with his father's lawyer. On this Tuesday morning, attired in an expensive three-piece gabardine suit, custom shirt, and tie from Napoleone, he announced to Emma that he would be spending the next several days in Triad's Manhattan office. Would she mind if he took the car?

Not at all, she replied. She'd be at the studio all day and wouldn't be needing it. She waited for his comment, but he made none.

They went their separate ways.

The Trent School of the Dance was not limited to ballet. It offered classes in modern dance, aerobics, and yoga. It catered to a diverse group of students, not just the boys from the high school athletic program. In the morning, the housewives came; after school, the children—little ones first, then the older ones. In the early evening, she got the after-work crowd, the lonely singles on their way home to lonely apartments. On Wednesdays she held a night class in tap dancing, from seven-thirty to nine. This was her favorite. This brought back memories of when she had been a performer.

The studio was on Queens Boulevard, just around the corner from the movie theater she'd attended on the night of the attack. It was on the fringe of the commercial area and occupied the entire second floor, with a private entrance at street level. The door opened directly on a narrow flight of stairs, which led only to the large, square rehearsal room. The usual *barre* ran around three sides and the walls were mirrored. There was a stereo and a stack of folding chairs in a corner. On the opposite side of the room a door opened onto Emma's small office. Another door led down a short corridor to the showers and lockers.

At a quarter of nine on Tuesday morning, Emma Trent took down the sign her neighbor, Sue Wanamaker, had tacked to the downstairs door, walked up the narrow flight of stairs, turned the key in the lock, and entered her domain. She put a new message on her answering machine to announce the school was back in operation.

Attendance was light that first day, but she reasoned it was because most of her pupils didn't know she was open. The word would spread, of course, she thought, and it did. Even as the day progressed, the number increased, till by evening there was a respectable attendance for aerobics.

Naturally, the children didn't say anything about what had happened, but Emma could tell by the way they looked at her that she had been the subject of discussion by their parents. The adults offered condolences and help—in whatever way she might require. Some even asked questions about the break-in and wanted to know what the police were doing.

"I haven't heard anything," she said.

Those who had been insensitive enough to ask were immediately contrite.

At closing time, several asked if she had plans and suggested she join them for dinner. She thanked them but declined. She was going to get a sandwich and go straight home and to bed, she said.

Everybody agreed it was the best thing. There was no doubt she had their sympathy and support.

It was what Emma had intended to do. She locked the upstairs door, walked down to the street, stepped outside and immediately noticed the car parked in front. Two men sat in it. She recognized one. "Hello, Sergeant Dixon."

He got out. "Can we give you a ride home, Mrs. Trent?"

Would it do any good to say no? she wondered. "Thank you."

"This is my partner, Detective Sackler," Dixon said as he held the rear door for her.

Emma Trent got in. She'd been expecting another visit, naturally, but not so soon, and her heart was pounding. Dixon closed the door and got back behind the wheel. No one spoke till they reached Clinton Place. Once again Ray Dixon got out and held the door for her.

"Do you want to come in?" she asked.

"It would be best."

As she walked up the path with the two detectives, Emma Trent felt the eyes of her neighbors on her. It was a relief to get inside. She didn't offer the detectives coffee or make any pretense at hospitality. She led the way to the dark and formal living room, sat down, and waited for whatever was to come.

Dixon got right to it. "We believe we have a lead to one of the persons who killed your husband."

A chill passed through her. She folded her hands in her lap and clenched them tightly to keep them from shaking.

"It's a boy from the neighborhood. A young adult, actually. He has a bad reputation. There are rumors he's involved in drugs." He watched closely for her reaction.

"I wouldn't know about that." She shrugged.

He tried again. "Your neighbor across the street, Mrs.

Wanamaker, observed this young man loitering around your house recently."

"She did? She never mentioned it to me."

"She behaved properly in coming to us first," Dixon said. "The boy's name is Paul Kellen, Junior. Do you know him?"

Emma Trent gasped. "Of course I know Paulie. He's in one of my dance classes. I give instruction to the members of several teams—basketball, hockey, baseball. It's part of the high school athletic program." She paused. "I can't believe..." She shook her head.

"How long has Kellen been taking..."

"Dance?" she finished for him. "I refer to it as *dance* rather than *ballet*. Calling it *ballet* would put the boys off."

"You were going to tell me how long Kellen has been a pupil."

"He started along with his team this past September."

"And how often does he come?"

"The team comes every week through the school year."

"And that's the only contact you have with him? In class?"

"Of course. What else?" She looked to Sackler as well.

"The boy lives not three blocks from you. I thought you and Mr. Trent might have socialized with his parents."

"No. I know who they are—respectable, financially secure. I know them by sight, that's all."

"Have you any idea why young Kellen might have broken into your house and attacked your husband?"

"My God, no! No idea. I can't imagine... You said whoever broke in probably needed money, but Paulie's a rich kid; his parents give him everything he wants."

Maybe not everything, Dixon thought. "Let's suppose that, for whatever reason, he needed cash. Why would he choose your house to burglarize?"

"I don't know."

"He must have thought the house was empty. What would have led him to believe that?"

She shook her head. "I might have mentioned that Douglas was going to be away, though I don't know why I would have spoken of it. God! If this happened because of some careless remark on my part, I'll never forgive myself. Never."

"He would also have had to know that you wouldn't be going directly home after class on Wednesday, that you were going to the movies. Did you happen to let that drop?"

She flushed. "I couldn't have. I didn't know myself. It was a spur-of-the-moment decision. I just didn't feel like going home to an empty house."

Dixon took a calculated pause. "Maybe it didn't matter whether you were home or not."

"You mean whoever it was was ready to kill me, too, if I got in the way? No. I've heard stories about Paulie Kellen—that he's wild, has a nasty temper. The kids are afraid of him. But I can't believe this. Have you talked to Paulie? What does he say?"

"What would you expect him to say? He denies everything. He claims he was home studying at the time."

"What do his parents say?"

"They back him up, of course."

"What do you expect me to tell you?"

For the first time since the interview began, Lew Sackler leaned forward to take part. "How did you and your husband get along, Mrs. Trent?"

"I've already answered that, but I'll answer it again. Fine. We got along just fine."

"Neither one of you was considering the possibility of divorce?"

"No! Where did you get that idea? Never mind, I know.

It was Jonathan." She sighed. "I have never been able to get him to accept me."

When Lew broke their date, Gwenn decided to stay home and make an early night of it. She put on a robe and slippers and watched television and waited for his call. He still hadn't called by ten. He would call in the morning, she decided, and went to bed.

In the morning, she picked up her copy of the *Daily News* waiting outside her door. The headlines told her why Lew had broken their date.

DANCE SCHOOL PUPIL QUESTIONED IN MURDER CASE
TEENAGER INTERROGATED IN BRUTAL KILLING
POLICE PROBE LINK TO MURDERED MAN'S WIFE

The story, however, was all the way back on page five. Though it was dressed up with a photograph of the elegant Trent house, the facts were meager and did not satisfy the expectations the front-page headlines had aroused.

The reader was assured their reporter was on top of the story and promised big developments. With the latest of the rape trials concluded and the primaries finished—at least those that would have any effect on the presidential nominations—news was thin. If there was anything at all to be gleaned on the case, the *News* could be counted on to squeeze out the last juicy drop.

Gwenn finished breakfast and still Lew hadn't called. Maybe there was nothing to call about; the interrogation had elicited nothing new. Or the interrogation had been successful and the results were being kept quiet. It wouldn't be for long, Gwenn thought; one reporter at least had caught the scent.

According to the forecast, there would be light showers

on and off for most of the day. Gwenn dressed accordingly: slacks, shirt, and a light trench coat. It was early and she made good time on the East River Drive till she got off into the local streets around City Hall. She lost a full twenty minutes because of a demonstration, one of the disadvantages of doing business in that part of town. It was ten-thirty when she entered her office.

Marge Pratt looked up. "I've called everywhere."

"Sorry," Gwenn apologized automatically. It was the easiest way. "What is it?"

"You had a call."

"From whom?"

"Mrs. Trent. Mrs. Emma Trent," she repeated, and waited for the reaction.

"What does she want?"

"She wants you to call back. Right away. That was over an hour ago."

"All right. Get her for me, will you?"

She barely had time to take off her coat and put it away when her phone rang.

"Ms. Ramadge? This is Emma Trent."

"Sorry to have kept you waiting, Mrs. Trent. What can I do for you?"

"You know about me?"

"I know what I read in the papers."

"Well, that's what I'd like to talk to you about. I would come to your office, but there are reporters watching the house. They'd follow me, and I'd just as soon they didn't know I'm consulting you. I wonder if you could come out to see me?"

"Well..."

"I understand it's an inconvenience, but I'll pay for your time. Please. I'd be very grateful."

Gwenn had a pretty good idea of what Mrs. Trent wanted and she didn't think it was a job for her. But she was excited to be called, and curious, too. "All right, Mrs. Trent. When would you like me to come?"

"As soon as possible. Right away, if you could manage it." She gave the address. "Maybe you should come around to the back. Though I suppose they're watching there, too."

There was an edge of despair to her voice. Gwenn felt sorry for her. "Don't worry, I'll get past them. Wait for me at the back. It should be about an hour."

Marge Pratt looked at Gwenn expectantly when she came out. "Are we on the case?" she asked.

Knowing it was very likely she'd get stuck in traffic on the Queensboro Bridge, Gwenn left the car in the lot and took the subway. She reached the Continental Avenue stop on the Independent just after one P.M. and emerged into ominous darkness. Lightning flashed across the sky back over Manhattan: out here, the rumbles of thunder were still faint. People milled on the streets, thronged the stores and restaurants. Except that the electric lights had to be turned on, nobody paid much attention to the warnings of nature. Gusts of wind picked up the litter and made churning whirlpools. Gwenn's eyes smarted from the grit. Following the directions Emma Trent had given, Gwenn crossed Austin Street and, passing under the arcades of Station Square, entered the Gardens.

It was as though she'd crossed the border into another country, an enclave of private streets and expensive homes. Despite discreet signs affixed to the old-fashioned lamp posts that warned parking was forbidden, cars were lined up on both sides of Clinton Place. Probably they belonged to the reporters Emma Trent had complained about.

Gwenn went around to the back and was halfway up the path to the kitchen door when a man with a camera came out from behind one of the cars and ran ahead of her to crouch and prepare to shoot.

Gwenn stopped where she was, smiled brightly, and posed.

"Is this for television? Am I going to be on TV?" she asked as a woman approached holding out a microphone.

"Television." The reply was automatic. "Who are you?" The smile was meaningless.

"Channel Two!" Gwenn exclaimed and pointed to the panel truck with the famed logo on the side. "Imagine that! Dan Rather's my favorite," she confided to the reporter. "I watch him all the time. But I've never seen you. Should I have? What's your name?"

"Rita Sayers. What's your business with Mrs. Trent?"

"Business?" Gwenn frowned. "Oh, I get you. You want to know what I'm doing here? I'm going to give her a massage."

"You come regularly, do you?" What a break! the TV reporter thought.

"Me? No. The regular girl is out sick, so they sent me."

"You don't know Mrs. Trent?"

"Nope. Never saw her before. So when am I going to be on TV? Tonight? On the six o'clock news?"

"Yes, that's right. The six o'clock news. Watch for it." The reporter had already turned away, motioning to her camera man that they were wasting their time.

Another reporter ran up. He pointed. "Who was that? What did you get?"

"Nothing. She's nobody."

Gwenn grinned and waved cheerfully. Without further interference, she walked up to the kitchen door and rang. The door was opened immediately and was closed as soon as she stepped inside.

"Thank you for coming," Emma Trent said.

"You're welcome."

They looked each other over.

"Would you mind if we talked in here?" Mrs. Trent asked. "My stepson is using the library and the living room is ... very exposed."

"Of course."

"I was just putting the kettle on for tea. Would you like some? Or coffee? Or something stronger?"

"Tea would be fine, thanks."

She gestured for Gwenn to take a chair at the kitchen table, but remained standing while the water in the kettle came to a boil.

The wind had blown the storm away to the east, and through a break in the clouds a rosy shaft of sun cast an aura around Emma Trent. It brought out the highlights in her light brown hair and imparted a tinge of color to her pale cheeks. She was wearing a black dress with long sleeves, the starkness relieved by a white organdy collar. Overly formal perhaps, but certainly becoming. It enhanced the classic nature of her beauty. She could have had her portrait painted in it. She was younger than she'd appeared in the current newspaper pictures, Gwenn thought, more like the photographs in Cordelia's file. Considering all she'd been through, that was surprising.

Emma Trent set out a pair of fine china cups, put a tea bag in each, and poured the boiling water. There was no attempt at any kind of ceremony. The woman was ill at ease in her own kitchen, Gwenn thought as she helped herself from the sugar bowl.

"What can I do for you, Mrs. Trent?"

"A Sergeant Dixon came to see me this morning. Apparently, one of my neighbors reported to him that she saw and recognized a certain teenager hanging around this house recently. It turns out he's in one of my dance classes."

Gwenn nodded.

"I hold a special class once a week for the boys on the

athletic teams of the local high school. Paulie Kellen is on one of those teams, the basketball team, I think. He also lives here, in the Gardens. I don't know anything else about him. Nothing."

"That's what you told Sergeant Dixon?"

"That's all I know."

"I don't see the problem."

"They're trying to forge a link between us!" Emma Trent exclaimed.

"Is there such a link?" Gwenn asked.

"Of course not. My God, of course not!"

"Then you have nothing to worry about."

"You don't think so?" Emma Trent demanded bitterly. "Then why didn't Sue Wanamaker, my neighbor from across the street, come to me with her story? She's supposed to be my friend. Why didn't she confide her suspicions to me instead of going to the police? I'll tell you why—because she believes I'm involved somehow. What's more, she hasn't kept it to herself. The word is out. I can feel it. They're talking about me, wondering ... my neighbors, my supposed friends, are avoiding me. In the supermarket or the post office, they look the other way when they see me. On the street, they cross to the other side. You saw the reporters out there; what do you suppose brought them?"

"Unfounded gossip." Gwenn shrugged. "About this Paulie Kellen, what does he say?"

"Nothing. As far as I know."

"If he'd incriminated you in any way, believe me, Mrs. Trent, you would have heard."

"I suppose so."

"Do the police have any evidence, real, hard, factual evidence to implicate you in your husband's death?"

"None. None."

"What's your motive supposed to have been?"

"I don't know."

Gwenn took a deep gulp of the oversweetened tea and then set the cup down firmly. "Unless you're honest and open with me, there's nothing I can do, Mrs. Trent. In fact, from what I can tell so far, what you really need is a good lawyer."

"Douglas and I signed a prenuptial agreement. The jist of it is—if he divorced me, I would get fifty thousand dollars for each year the marriage had lasted. If I divorced him, I got nothing."

"Was a divorce in the offing?"

"Not that I know of."

Gwenn stifled her exasperation. "We're spinning our wheels here, Mrs. Trent. Once again, you've got to be straight with me."

Emma Trent clenched her teeth as though something might slip through against her will. After a few moments she relaxed. "Douglas never spoke of divorce."

Not exactly a ringing denial, Gwenn thought. "But you weren't getting along?"

Finally, she admitted, "No."

"Certainly, you were in no position to divorce him." Gwenn paused for emphasis. "As his widow, however, you're sitting pretty."

"I resent that, Miss Ramadge. I didn't expect this attitude from you."

"It's how the police will look at it as soon as they find out. And they will, you can depend on it. As Douglas Trent's divorced wife you would have got a hundred thousand dollars based on two years of marriage. As his widow, you get everything. Unless, of course, you're implicated in his murder. Then you get nothing. You cannot profit from your crime."

"I didn't do it. I have an alibi."

"From what I hear, that alibi isn't exactly watertight. At this stage, it doesn't matter. What's important now is what this Paulie Kellen says. Unless he admits he committed the crime and then goes on to claim you put him up to it, you've got nothing to worry about. And you certainly don't need me."

"Wait. Please. I do need you. This all goes back to an old scandal that happened before I married Douglas. It was never proved nor disproved, but it hangs over me. If you could show I was innocent there, then I'm sure all these other suspicions would be cleared away."

"You're talking about the death of your first husband."

Mrs. Trent nodded. "The situations are similar."

"Yes and no. In any case, there are rigid requirements before a past crime is admissible into evidence. And you were never charged." Gwenn's mind churned as she recited automatically, "The crime may not be cited by police or prosecutor or referred to without the court's permission." So that was why Emma Trent had called her. "It's very difficult to prove a negative. My partner, Cordelia Hart, couldn't do it when your husband went to her before your marriage. After all this time, I certainly can't. I'm sorry. But it's really not necessary." Gwenn picked up her hand bag and rose, but she didn't leave. Something about Emma Trent touched her. She was under fire from every direction—from the police, the media, her stepson and his family, and now also from her past. Cordelia had believed in her, and that counted heavily with Gwenn.

"Do you have any family of your own, Mrs. Trent?"

"My parents died in a plane crash."

Gwenn recalled the file. "There's nobody else?"

"Don't worry about me, Miss Ramadge. I'll get by. If you'll send me a bill—and don't forget your travel time..."

The front doorbell rang. They heard the door being opened and the sound of voices. Then Jonathan Trent looked in.

"A couple of detectives want to see you," he announced. "One of them was here this morning, Sergeant Dixon."

"This is my stepson, Jonathan. Miss Ramadge." Without further explanation, Emma Trent started down the hall to the front entrance and they trailed along.

Ray Dixon's eyes opened wide when he saw Gwenn. "Well, Miss Ramadge, this is a surprise."

"I didn't expect to see you either, Sergeant. Or you, Detective Sackler."

Lew just raised his eyes to the heavens.

"What are you doing here?" Dixon asked politely.

"I'm a private investigator. I'm investigating."

Lew covered his mouth.

Jonathan Trent, however, jumped in. "Investigating what?"

"That's confidential."

Emma Trent's amber eyes filled. She swallowed. When she spoke, the tears were gone and her voice was steady. "You wanted to see me?" she asked the detectives.

Dixon answered. "We wanted to advise you that your husband's remains are being released. You may go ahead with funeral arrangements."

"Thank you. It was kind of you to come and tell me in person."

"To be honest with you, Mrs. Trent, there's another reason," Dixon admitted. "We've recovered the murder weapons."

Gwenn watched the blood drain out of Emma Trent's already pale face.

Jonathan Trent found a chair to sit in. "You mean, what they used to beat him?"

"Yes. Two baseball bats."

"Two..." Trent echoed.

Dixon nodded. "From the beginning we were inclined to believe there were two perpetrators. Mr. Trent was a big man, physically fit. One attacker alone would have had to hit a particularly vicious and accurate blow to stun him and render him defenseless against the savage beating that ensued. The discovery of the two bats confirms our suspicions," he continued. "So does the attempt to get rid of the bats. One of the perpetrators tried to burn them, but he was seen. A man on his way home from work spotted the fire and reported it. The perpetrator got away, but the fire department recovered the bats and turned them over to us. We sent them to the lab for analysis. Through DNA testing, they determined that the blood which had soaked into the wood was that of Douglas Trent." Dixon paused. "Unfortunately, there was no other physical evidence."

"Two bats . . ." Jonathan Trent murmured in the ensuing silence and looked straight at his stepmother.

Emma Trent's eyes closed. She swayed. Gwenn and the two detectives reached out for her.

Chapter ———————————

———————— SEVEN

"Do you honestly believe that Emma Trent wielded one of those bats?" Gwenn Ramadge asked.

She had accepted a lift to the subway and was riding in front with Ray Dixon while Lew sat in the back.

"Do you really believe that she not only conspired but participated with a teenage boy in the murder of her husband? That she raised a baseball bat and brought it down on his head over and over and over till it was a bloody pulp? Till his brains oozed out? Can you see her doing that?"

"I think she knows who did it."

"That was a nasty way to try to find out," Gwenn accused.

"What we have here is a pretty nasty case."

"You're right, of course," she acknowledged and was silenced for a while. "Are you sure you're not influenced by the fact that she's going to inherit a lot of money and by the suspicions attached to her first husband's death?"

"Are you sure you're not influenced by your partner's investigation and her conclusion?" Dixon countered.

"I can't ignore it."

"I'm not ignoring it, either," he told her. "I'm putting a different interpretation on it."

They rode past the silent and empty tennis stadium.

Though no longer in use, it was still a prestigious land-mark for the neighborhood, a reminder of past glories. A right turn on Yellowstone brought them to the station house.

"You can let me out here," Gwenn said. "It's only a couple of blocks to the subway."

"Whatever you say." Dixon pulled over.

"It would be interesting to know where the perp stashed those bats in the interval between the murder and the time of the fire," she remarked.

"Any idea how to find out?" Dixon asked.

"Not yet."

Lew got out and opened the door for her. "I'll call you."

Dixon looked from one to the other. "If anything occurs to you, or if you uncover any new evidence, you will share it, won't you, Miss Ramadge?"

"Will you do the same for me?"

"Insofar as we're able."

"Same goes for me, Sergeant." She got out. "Thanks for the lift."

They watched her till she was lost in the crowd.

"You two known each other a long time?" Dixon asked.

"A year. Maybe a little more."

"Serious?"

"Not till lately."

So, Dixon thought. Just as well to find out early on. Anyway, he generally avoided career women, particu-larly police women. If the woman was working for him, he found himself reaffirming his right to authority. If she outranked him, he felt constrained to follow orders with-out question. Of course, a PI wasn't a police officer, but it was close enough. On the other hand, his ex-wife, Patty, had been strictly a homebody, and that hadn't worked.

"You could do worse," he told Sackler.

While Dixon went around the corner to park, Sackler entered the station house.

The next morning, Gwenn had Marge Pratt mail one of their standard contracts to Emma Trent. The secretary's eyes were bright. She didn't comment or ask questions, but Gwenn knew she was excited to be involved in such a big case. For her own part, Gwenn was uneasy, not because of the publicity the case was getting, but because it was a homicide—a brutal and violent one. A teenager was the prime suspect. Her client was under suspicion as the instigator or an actual participant. It didn't get much worse, she thought as she stood at her window and stared out at the drab facade of City Hall. In spite of all that and in spite of her determination not to take any more homicide cases, she decided to go ahead. It was a reaction to the readiness of the police to accept Emma Trent's guilt and the general antagonism toward her. Ray Dixon had accused Gwenn of being influenced by Cordelia's favorable report.

It was true. But it wasn't all. There was something about Ray Dixon that challenged her and made her want to show off, she admitted. It could be because of his name. The one serious love affair she'd ever had had been with a man named Ray. Ray Eagan. He was the only man who had ever dominated her. She had been so totally dependent on him, and maybe now she was trying to show . . . herself through this other Ray, that she didn't need him? That she could stand on her own two feet? She'd implied she could find out where those bats had been kept between Wednesday night and Thursday night, but there was no way of doing so without first knowing who had used them. Someone besides her client must have had a motive for wanting to get rid of Douglas Trent. There were others besides Emma Trent who would profit from his death: members of his family, friends, business associates.

She called Triad Paper to make an appointment with Jonathan Trent.

"I thought you were working for my stepmother." Trent made no effort to mask his antagonism. "Talking to me won't do you any good. Whether or not she took part, she's morally guilty of my father's murder. I'm not going to help you clear her. Besides, I wasn't even here, so I can't tell you anything."

"Suppose she's not responsible? Don't you want the guilty party found and punished?"

"Of course." He sighed with exasperation. "All right. My family is coming down for the funeral. They're due this afternoon, and I'm meeting them at the airport. If you want to come around to the house later in the evening, say about eight-thirty . . . ?"

"I'll be there, Mr. Trent. Thank you."

This time it was Gwenn who canceled the dinner date.

"Sorry, Lew. It's the only time he could give me. I had no choice."

"Sure, but you're wasting your efforts. Jonathan Trent was in Toronto when the crime was committed."

"You're willing to accept that Emma Trent could have hired someone to do the murder. If she could, why couldn't Jonathan, or somebody else?"

"No reason. So call me when you're through."

"I have no idea when that will be."

"Okay. Want to make it tomorrow? We could go to the ballgame; there's a twilight doubleheader."

Gwenn arrived at Clinton Place promptly at eight-thirty that evening. She found the situation very different from what it had been the day before. The reporters were gone; called to something more interesting, she thought as she walked up the path to the front door without anyone to challenge her. She rang the bell, and a maid in uniform answered. Inside, the gloom had been dispelled. There was no longer a sense of being under siege. Every light was on. The television blared. As the maid led Gwenn to the living room, they passed the open dining room and she noted the table. Six places had been laid. They had not yet been cleared.

As soon as he saw her, Jonathan Trent went to greet her. While not cordial, he was at least not openly surly. "Sheila, this is Miss Ramadge, Miss Ramadge, my wife."

Sheila Trent was older than both her husband and her mother-in-law, well into her thirties. She was tall, with a narrow face and raven curls and light eyes set too closely together. It made her look suspicious, constantly probing. Not an easy woman to live with, Gwenn surmised as she acknowledged the introduction.

From her five foot nine, Sheila Trent looked down on Gwenn Ramadge.

"Our children, John, Mary, Phyllis," he called out sternly.

The boy was about six. He took after his mother, dark and lanky. The girls, possibly three and four, were pudgy replicas of their father. Each in turn acknowledged Gwenn for a brief moment and then returned to the television. Nobody, and that included the parents, made a move to lower the volume, much less turn the set off. It was not exactly a house of mourning, Gwenn thought. And where was the lady of the house? Where was her client?

"Is there somewhere we can talk?" she asked, raising her voice.

"The library."

He led the way and his wife fell in behind. Evidently she intended to be present during the interview. Well, why not? It might even turn out to be useful.

Once the door was closed and they were seated, Jonathan Trent wasted no time. "Well, Miss Ramadge?"

She followed his lead. "I'd like to clarify the relationship between you and your father and his second wife."

"You already know that Sheila and I disapproved of the marriage and we tried in every way possible to stop it. My father was obsessed with Emma Brodsky Bliss Hailey, whatever her name was. He wouldn't hear a word against her. He hired your agency to investigate her, but he wasn't interested in finding out the truth. He only wanted to pacify us. It's my opinion he said as much to your Ms. Hart and that the report she submitted followed his wishes."

Gwenn flushed. Her green eyes threw off sparks. "Miss Hart would not turn in a biased report."

"No, of course not," Sheila Trent intervened. "I'm sure Ms. Hart was totally honest and did the best she could."

She hadn't made it any better, and Gwenn wasn't sure she'd meant to. She decided not to pursue the matter now, but she wasn't going to forget it.

"How did you feel about your father-in-law marrying a second time?" she asked Sheila Trent.

"I thought the same as Jonathan—that she was marrying Douglas for his money."

"Money which would otherwise in due course have come to you."

"That's right."

"But you're well off, aren't you? Your husband holds a good position in his father's company. He's well paid. And I suppose he's not forgotten in the will."

"Naturally," Jonathan stepped in. "I am my father's only child. I don't know the details of the will, but I expect to be remembered. There'll be a reading of the will after the funeral."

"The name of your father's lawyer?"

"George LeBrun."

Gwenn made a note.

"This last trip of your father's up to Toronto, it was part of a regular schedule of visits to the Canadian offices? A general review of how things were going?"

"That's right."

"How often did he come?"

"Three or four times a year."

"What was the date of the trip prior to this one?"

"Ah . . . I think he came up in early May."

Gwenn frowned. "According to Mrs. Emma Trent, it was mid-May. Why did he go back a scant two weeks later? What was wrong?"

"Nothing was wrong. Nothing. In fact, to the contrary. We were negotiating to buy a tract of timberland. He came up for the negotiations."

"I see. From whom were you buying the land?"

"We're not prepared to release that information."

"I'm not looking to trade on it," Gwenn assured him. "All I'm interested in is the reason for your father's precipitous return."

"It wasn't precipitous. I've told you why he came up."

"To participate in the negotiations, yes. Were they successful?"

"That's none of your business."

"Which means they weren't. Things were not going well and your father went up to help, but it was too late. The deal had already fallen through. There was nothing he could do to salvage it, so he came back—a day early."

"He could have come back for the opposite reason—because the negotiations had been concluded, successfully," Trent suggested.

"Then why would you be trying so hard to hide the fact?"

"That's enough!" Sheila Trent broke in. "I don't know what you think you're doing or what Emma told you, but I can assure you of one thing: the bond between Jonathan and his father was strong and she was jealous of it. Douglas was also devoted to our children, his grandchildren, and she was jealous of them, too. When he came to Toronto, he stayed with us but she never accompanied him. And if she told you that his father was not satisfied with Jonathan's job performance, that's a lie, too."

"You're the first one to mention that possibility," Gwenn told her.

Sheila Trent flushed darkly, then recovered. "It happens that Douglas was very pleased with Jonathan and had promised him a raise."

"I see." Gwenn nodded. There was nothing more to be learned here. Not now. "Is Mrs. Trent at home?"

"She's at her studio." Sheila Trent's lips were stretched thin in disapproval.

Passing the open living room on her way out, Gwenn was again assaulted by the blare of the television. The children were sprawled on the floor in front of it eating popcorn and drinking Cokes. The cans left rings on the polished tabletops; crayons meant for coloring books streaked the light beige carpet. Emma Trent could very well have escaped to the dance studio merely to have some quiet, to be able to nurture her grief, Gwenn thought. She considered dropping in on her, but there was nothing new to report or discuss. She headed back to the city.

At home, Gwenn changed into an old pair of slacks and a T-shirt. She kicked off her shoes and put on house slippers. She fixed herself an egg salad on rye and a cup of instant decaf. Then, while the recent interview was still fresh in her mind, she typed up her notes. It was midnight when she went to bed. She fell asleep immediately.

When she awoke, the sun was an orange globe peeping

over the horizon. By the time she'd showered and had breakfast it was yellow and high in a cloudless sky, shimmering on the placid waters of the East River. From the back of her closet, Gwenn brought out her good black Chanel suit with the beige trim. She made a face as she held it up to herself. She didn't look well in black and she didn't like wearing it, but there were certain occasions that demanded it and a funeral was certainly one of them.

It was a bad day for a funeral, Gwenn thought. To bury a loved one on a day when nature flaunted the glory of life only intensified the pain. Of course, not all who would attend today would be there out of genuine sorrow.

About thirty persons were present at the funeral mass at Our Lady Queen of Martyrs Church on Queens Boulevard. They were all but lost in it. However, almost all went out to the cemetery for the interment. That suggested Douglas Trent had inspired affection. Or else someone was a good organizer. Gwenn, driving in her own car, joined the cortege of hired limousines. Passing through the cemetery gates, she was impressed by the park-like environs. There were rolling lawns, fine straight oak trees, a variety of pines. Dogwoods and magnolias were in full bloom. The procession wound along the perimeter and came to a stop opposite a quiet pond upon which swans glided serenely. The mourners stepped from the cars and formed a circle around the open grave. The casket was lifted from the hearse and set at one side. The minister approached and began to read the familiar psalm:

"Yea, though I walk through the valley of the shadow of death . . ."

Bowing her head, Gwenn watched surreptitiously and tried to read the reactions of those around her.

Jonathan and Sheila Trent, minus the children, stood at one side of the casket. Maurice Jessup, Douglas Trent's business partner, and his wife took positions opposite.

Gwenn could identify Jessup because he had given the eulogy. She knew who the woman with him was because she'd asked.

Jessup, though well into his sixties, was still a handsome man. Ruddy faced, with a sharp nose and a lean, hard jawline, he gave the initial impression of vigor and physical strength. He carried himself with the assurance of success. On closer scrutiny, it could be seen despite the efforts of an expensive tailor that his left arm was withered and special shoes could not compensate for a mangled left foot.

Helen Jessup was a plump, matronly woman with snow-white hair, rigidly coiffed and sprayed to stay that way. She was smart enough not to try to be stylish. She was what she was and she stood proudly beside her man.

At the head of the casket, between the two groups that had ranged themselves behind Jonathan Trent and Maurice Jessup, was the widow. A black veil covered Emma Trent's face.

When the minister delivered the final blessing, the casket was lowered into the ground. The ceremonial spadeful of earth thrown over it completed the ritual. The mourners turned toward the waiting cars. But it wasn't over, Gwenn thought. They could turn their backs on Douglas Trent and walk away, but they could not forget him or the past. They couldn't look to the future. Not yet.

Gwenn watched as Emma Trent, with the Jessups and Jonathan and Sheila on either side, prepared to receive one last round of condolences. She was looking for an unusual reaction, though she didn't know exactly what. So far, everything appeared normal. She had expected that either Lew or Sergeant Dixon might be present, but she hadn't seen either one. They probably thought their time would be better spent elsewhere.

Gwenn Ramadge was one of the few persons who had

her own transportation and was not part of a group. But there was someone else who had come alone. She was tall and slim and she wore a black suit much like Gwenn's—and everyone else's for that matter. She topped her costume with a wide-brimmed black straw hat that shadowed her face and covered her hair. To complete the disguise she wore dark glasses. However, instead of rendering her anonymous, the getup aroused curiosity. She hadn't attended the mass, of that Gwenn was certain. And now, while the mourners dispersed and got into the cars that would take them back to the city, the woman remained. She watched while the grave diggers continued their work. When the casket was covered, she turned and headed on foot toward the cemetery exit.

Leaving her car where it was, Gwenn followed.

She followed the woman out of the grounds, then down the hill to Queens Boulevard where she flagged a cab and got in. The light changed. There were other cabs, plenty of them, and Gwenn ran out into the street to get one. As she did so, a limousine cut in front of her.

A black-tinted window was lowered.

"Need a lift, Miss Ramadge?" Jonathan Trent asked.

She stood helplessly and watched as the light changed back to green and the taxi crossed the intersection and merged into traffic.

"No, thanks. I have my car."

Joyce Hazzlit gave the driver her address and then fell back against the seat.

It was over. Finished. At last, after all these years, she was safe. When the phone rang she would no longer have to be afraid to pick it up. When she put her key in the lock and opened her own front door, she could be sure he wouldn't be sitting there waiting for her. She could accept bookings confident that she wouldn't have to cancel at the last minute because she wasn't in condition to work.

Behind the dark glasses, her gray eyes filled and the tears coursed over the sculptured planes of her face. She cried quietly, not out of regret or sorrow. She cried out of relief.

Chapter
EIGHT

The gold lettering on the plate-glass door read: THE TRIAD BUILDING. The title was more impressive than the edifice, which was a narrow, six-story, pre-war building much in need of renovation. Nevertheless, the location in the heart of mid-town Manhattan was prime. If Triad did indeed own, rather than lease, the building, it would add considerably to the value of Douglas Trent's estate.

Gwenn walked into the executive offices promptly at nine on Monday morning. She recognized the receptionist as one of the mourners at the funeral, one who had cried copiously. She stated her business and handed over one of her cards. Then she took a seat and prepared to wait.

She'd barely settled when a matronly woman, whose dyed red hair couldn't hide she was close to sixty, came out. She took the card from the receptionist, studied it, then looked Gwenn over.

"I'm May Danneford, Mr. Jessup's secretary. Mr. Jessup is tied up just now. As you can imagine, we're in considerable turmoil. Perhaps I could help you?"

She had been at the funeral too, Gwenn recalled, but she hadn't done much crying.

"That's very kind of you." Secretaries and assistants were often flattered to be accepted as sources of information in place of the boss. Miss Danneford's manner suggested she might be like that. "The problem is I need to ask some questions about the partnership, and you might prefer not to get involved."

That put a brake on Miss Danneford's eagerness. "I'll speak to Mr. Jessup. You might have to come back at a later time."

"Whenever it's convenient." Gwenn returned to her seat, but she didn't have to wait long this time, either.

"Mr. Jessup is very busy, but as long as you're here, he'll see you. This way."

The secretary led Gwenn down the length of the corridor into a smaller reception area. Two doors opened off it: one was marked Maurice Jessup, the other, Douglas Trent. Twin executive suites, Gwenn thought. She followed Danneford into the anteroom of the Jessup offices. It was small but boasted a floor-to-ceiling window through which daylight poured. Plants of various species and sizes flourished. On a long credenza, photographs were displayed: family pictures. May Danneford must have been working for Jessup for a very long time to be so confidently entrenched.

Danneford tapped at her boss's door. "Miss Ramadge, sir," she announced, stepped aside, and then left.

While delivering the eulogy, he had been dignified. Later, beside the grave, he had appeared dour. But now, in his own domain, he was gracious. Rising, he stretched a hand out across the desk, his dark eyes fixed on her with real interest. Holding her card in his left hand, he studied it, then put it down with an awkward but practiced gesture.

"So you're a private eye." He waved her to a chair. "What can I do for you?"

"I'm investigating Mr. Trent's death."

"I thought the police had decided it was attempted burglary."

"There are other possibilities. I'm looking into them."

"Ah . . ." he considered. "And who's paying you? Excuse me for being blunt, Miss Ramadge, but I assume you're not doing this just because you're a good citizen."

"True," she admitted. "I don't see any harm in telling you. I'm working for Mrs. Trent. Mrs. Emma Trent. She wants her husband's killer or killers found and convicted."

"And why have you come to me?" Now he was not quite so affable.

"I'm looking for a possible motive."

"A motive that would apply to me?"

"Not specifically. I do have to explore the situation here at Triad. I understand that Douglas Trent paid an unscheduled visit to the Toronto office, which is under the management of his son, Jonathan. Apparently, a very important land deal had turned sour."

"There was a problem," Jessup admitted. "I don't know what. Doug went up to find out."

"He came back a day sooner than expected. Why?"

"I have no idea."

"You weren't in touch? He didn't advise you of his progress, or notify you that he was coming back early?"

"He couldn't. I was at my place in Virginia Beach. We'd had a big storm and power was out for several days. Telephones were down. Communications were restored early on Thursday, the sixth. That's when his secretary, Rachel Montrone, finally got through to me to tell me he was coming back and wanted to see me. He also wanted the accountant."

"That was the storm that was supposed to hit New York and then bypassed us?"

"No, it was another, a week earlier, a big ocean disturbance."

In the guise of forthrightness, Maurice Jessup had also

provided himself with an alibi, Gwenn noted. "Did he say why he wanted you and the accountant?"

"No. But according to Rachel, he was very agitated."

"How long were you and Douglas Trent in business together?"

"We go back a long way." He stretched out his legs and slid down in the chair. "We worked together as lumberjacks in the Canadian forests."

That explained a lot that had puzzled her. Corporate polish could not completely obliterate the logging camp. She had a feeling that Maurice Jessup didn't want to forget his origins, that he actually cherished them. He confirmed her hunch by abruptly getting up and walking over to the far wall and a group of pictures that hung there. He picked out one. It showed about a dozen men in work clothes and hard hats standing in front of a cabin in the woods.

He pointed. "That's me."

There were more lines in his face and some gray in his hair, but otherwise he hadn't changed much. She would have been able to pick him out of the group easily.

"That's Douglas," he pointed.

Douglas Trent was shorter and stockier. He had a wide, bold face. His features were thick, shoulders and chest heavy. She could imagine him swinging his axe to bring down those towering, majestic trees. She realized suddenly that until that moment she'd had no idea what Douglas Trent looked like. The casket had been closed during the wake and the funeral. Until now no one had offered to show her a picture. No pictures had been displayed in his house. It occurred to her that no one had expressed regret that Douglas Trent was gone. No one had said: we'll miss him. That included his son and daughter-in-law. It included Emma Trent.

"We both worked for Triad." Jessup was lost in nostalgia. "I had an accident. We were doing some reforestation and I was lubricating the manure spreader. My clothes got snagged and my foot and arm caught in the machine. I was lucky the major arteries and nerves to my leg and hand were spared. They patched me up, but I had to get out of the camp. I went into management. Doug got out too; he married the boss's daughter."

Gwenn's eyes widened. "The first Mrs. Trent?"

"Lucille. That's right."

"Her father founded the company and she inherited it?"

"Not all of it. The old man knew she'd put Doug in charge. Doug was a good salesman and a good PR man, but when it came to running operations... let's just say he wasn't qualified. So Mr. Franklin left forty percent of Triad to me, figuring I'd keep a steady hand on the helm."

"How long ago was all this?"

"Well, he and Emma were married about two years. Lucille's father died fifteen years before she did. Make it between seventeen and eighteen years."

"That you've been in business together? How has it worked out?"

Slowly, with his characteristically uneven gait, Jessup went back to his desk. "Pretty much as the old man figured it would. Oh, we had our disagreements from time to time, but we resolved them."

Gwenn nodded. "Triad has a good reputation. I've asked around. You run a tight ship."

"Thanks."

"I understand you're going to show an increase in earnings for the year. The Canadian operation, however, isn't doing so well."

"There have been problems," Jessup admitted. "Recent fires have destroyed entire tracts. We were negotiating to buy additional timberland in order to be able to fill orders."

"Jonathan Trent was in charge of that?"

Jessup nodded.

"Is he competent?"

The partner hesitated. "Under supervision."

"Is he honest?"

"As far as I know."

Not a glowing testimonial, Gwenn thought. "You said that when Douglas Trent called to set up the meeting for Thursday, he also ordered his secretary to get hold of the accountant. Could he have uncovered some financial irregularity up there in Toronto?"

Jessup hesitated. His lean, grave face was troubled. "I wouldn't want to guess."

"But, of course, you will investigate."

"You can be sure."

Gwenn took a deep breath and addressed another aspect. "I assume that Mrs. Emma Trent inherits her husband's share of the business."

"No. It goes to Jonathan."

"Really? Is this a provision of Douglas Trent's will?"

"It was a condition of the first Mrs. Trent's will. She was the majority stockholder in Triad. She could approve or disapprove any action or policy. She seldom did, though. She never meddled. I'm sure you know that she suffered a very long and painful illness. She was concerned about what would happen to the company her father had labored so hard to build. I suppose she anticipated that Doug would remarry and she wanted to make sure that in case of his death, the company would not go to a stranger. She was also naturally concerned that her son would be provided for. Actually, Doug wasn't much more than a caretaker for Jonathan."

"Does Emma Trent know this?"

"I couldn't say."

"How about Jonathan?"

"Miss Ramadge, I don't know. Doug did not confide

in me. My guess, if you're interested, is no. Lucille was very anxious for her son to stand on his own feet. Telling him that he had big money coming would defeat the purpose. As for Doug, he would lose what control he had over Jonathan."

With the major part of the business passing on to the son, what would be left for Emma? "Mr. Trent's first marriage appears to have been very successful. How about the second? Were he and Emma happy?"

He took his time answering. "My wife, Helen, and Lucille were very close. While we both appreciated that Lucille's long illness was an ordeal for Doug as well as for her, his remarrying so quickly after her death and to such a young woman...it upset Helen. She made no secret of it. We didn't attend the wedding and we didn't socialize with them afterwards."

"Did the rest of Lucille Trent's friends react in that way?"

"They did."

"That was hardly Emma's fault," Gwenn commented.

"I didn't say it was. I had no quarrel with Emma Trent," he retorted sharply.

It caught Gwenn up short. "I'm sorry. I didn't mean to blame you." She had gone far enough, for this session anyway. She rose and held out her hand.

"Thank you for seeing me. You've given me a lot to think about."

When Gwenn came out, Miss Danneford was nowhere to be seen. She could find her way out, of course, no problem, but she hesitated. She was right there in front of Douglas Trent's door. It wouldn't hurt to take a quick look around, she thought. She tapped lightly. Getting no answer, she walked in.

The office was small, the twin of May Danneford's, but the character was completely different. There was no display of personal photographs, no plants, no clutter. It looked like a furnished room waiting to be rented. The door to the inner office was slightly, invitingly, ajar. Gwenn eased it open and peered inside.

A woman stood at the window looking out. Gwenn cleared her throat.

"Good morning."

The woman turned. "Yes?"

Because of the backlighting her face remained in shadow. "You're Rachel Montrone, Mr. Trent's secretary, right? My name is Gwenn Ramadge. I'm investigating his death." She held out one of her cards.

In order to get the light on it, Rachel Montrone turned sideways and in so doing revealed herself. She, too, must be close to forty, Gwenn thought, and still beautiful. She was a *soft* woman; buxom, not fat; skin very white and without blemish, the kind of skin that bruised easily. Her chestnut hair was abundant, threaded with gray. She wore no makeup except around the eyes and that was artfully done with two shades of eye shadow. The current fashion of short, tight skirts was often unkind to those over thirty, but Miss Montrone managed to be in style without appearing ludicrous.

Having read the card, the secretary looked up. "I thought the police had a suspect."

"They do. I'm working for Mrs. Trent."

"Mrs. Trent hired you?"

"That's right."

"Why?"

"To make sure the police get the right person."

"Well." She walked past Gwenn and out to her own desk and sat down. "What can I do for you?"

Everybody asked, Gwenn thought following, but nobody really wanted to help. "You've been with Mr. Trent a long time."

"Eighteen years. Eighteen good years. I came to work

for Mr. Trent and Mr. Jessup when they came down from Canada and opened the original office in Brooklyn. That was right after old Mr. Franklin died. I was receptionist, clerk, and secretary to the two of them. I was the entire office staff. When we started to expand, I became supervisor, then office manager. Finally, I switched to working exclusively for Mr. Trent as his executive secretary."

"You've come a long way together."

"Yes."

"His death must have been a terrible blow for you."

She nodded.

Gwenn waited for some sort of tribute, but Rachel Montrone didn't add anything. "Are you satisfied with the police conclusion that the attack was a result of a burglary gone out of control?"

"What else could it have been?"

It was not a rhetorical question, Gwenn realized with surprise. The secretary expected an answer. Gwenn couldn't give one.

"You knew Mrs. Lucille Trent, of course."

"Lucille was a wonderful person. Her father founded the company, but she never threw her weight around, never lorded it over anybody. She was kind and understanding."

"So you must have been surprised when Douglas Trent married again so soon after her death."

"Yes. We all were." She sighed. "Surprised and shocked. At first. Then we realized how very lonely he must have been, and how vulnerable. Despite Lucille's long illness, she'd been a very big part of his life. Her death left a void. He thought he was prepared for it, but one can never fully anticipate or prepare for such a loss."

"You must have been surprised he married such a young woman," Gwenn persisted.

The secretary continued to defend her boss. "Again,

it was a matter of putting oneself in his place. It was her youth that attracted him. Her youth and energy that he needed. After so many years of being restricted to a sick room, after so many years of standing with Lucille at death's edge, Emma dragged him back to life."

Gwenn had not expected a defense of Emma Trent from this source, certainly not such a sensitive and sympathetic one. "According to Jonathan and Sheila Trent, the marriage was in trouble."

Rachel Montrone raised eyebrows. "He didn't confide in me."

"Surely after all these years you knew Douglas Trent well enough to sense how things were at home for him."

"Well, he was unhappy. I could see that." She paused. "Maybe disappointed is a better way of putting it, but he never said a word against her. To be fair, I don't think it was working out for either of them. My feeling is that neither one found what he was looking for in the marriage. That's why Emma started the dance school—to fill a void. Mr. Trent thought it took up too much of her time. He didn't like coming home at night to an empty house. You can't blame him."

"So he did complain to you."

"Only about the school."

Gwenn shifted the focus. "How well do you know Emma Trent?"

"Not at all. Mr. Trent brought her into the office once, right after they were married. He introduced her around, and that was it."

"She didn't drop by from time to time?" Rachel Montrone shook her head. "Didn't pick him up to go to lunch? Never called to speak to her husband, to leave messages, to ask you to do errands?"

"She didn't do any of those things."

"Unusual, wouldn't you say?"

"I thought it was considerate."

"As far as you know, then, the only disagreement between them concerned the dance school. Was that serious enough to make them think of divorce?"

Rachel Montrone hesitated longer than she had at any other question. Finally, she found an answer. She stiffened. Her soft eyes gleamed with a hard, sharp light. "They'd only been married a couple of years. They were still adjusting."

Chapter ————————————
————————— NINE

The basketball team was scheduled for a class at the Trent Dance Studio at four P.M. on Tuesday as usual. A bus was provided to take them from the school in Jamaica to Forest Hills for the session and then return them to their homes. Lew Sackler and Ray Dixon parked across the street and watched as the boys filed by.

They were looking for one particular student, Paulie Kellen, the boy Sue Wanamaker reported she had seen loitering around the Trent house several days before Douglas Trent's murder. They'd already interrogated Kellen. They'd asked him what he'd been doing at the Trent house. Paulie had simply denied being there. Very politely. He was from a good family—affluent, privileged. He'd been brought up to be courteous to his elders and teachers, to respect authority. He was tall and good looking with tawny gold hair swept back from a wide brow and blue eyes that could express innocent bewilderment with ease. And he was very sure of himself. He'd suggested to the detectives, managing to be both respectful and disparaging at the same time, that Mrs. Wanamaker's vision wasn't very good, and, poor thing, she was known to get muddled. He concluded that she'd seen somebody else who looked like him.

Why should he have been hanging around the Trent

place? he'd asked, turning the problem back on the detectives.

Had he had business with Mr. Trent or Mrs. Trent? Dixon asked.

What kind of business? Paulie wanted to know.

They asked him what he'd been doing on the night of Wednesday, June fifth.

He'd been home studying for an exam. Why not ask his parents, if they didn't believe him?

The detectives did ask Mr. and Mrs. Kellen, who confirmed their son had been at home studying just as he said. They refused to discuss the matter further.

They couldn't be forced.

There wasn't enough probable cause to request a search warrant. For now, all Sackler and Dixon could do was watch the teenager and hope he would make a mistake. He was only a kid, after all. But time was running out. The captain was satisfied with the random break-in theory and was ready to close the book on the case.

While they waited for the bus to load and pull out, the two detectives observed the general pattern of activity. Drug dealing was epidemic through the school system. A campaign diligently pursued by parents and police had resulted in clearing out pushers at least in a proscribed area around school property. Once the students went beyond that, it was not possible to protect them. As far as Sackler and Dixon could tell, the buffer zone around this particular school remained effective. They could spot no transactions.

In due course, Paulie Kellen came down the steps and got on the bus. Full at last, it pulled out and the detectives followed. It was a short trip. The bus double-parked in front of the studio and let the boys out. They entered the building directly. No one dawdled. Once empty, the bus drove off.

The class was scheduled to last an hour and a half.

The detectives waited. Time passed. The boys were on
time coming out; the bus was late to pick them up. They
milled on the sidewalk pummeling each other, indulging
in high-spirited horse play. At the edge of all this activity
a tall, gangly youth in jeans and a bombardier jacket
somehow materialized. As the bus appeared and came
toward them, the youth stepped off the curb between two
parked cars where he couldn't be observed by the driver
or the boys—not unless they happened to be looking for
him. One of them, at least, was.

The detectives got out of their car and went over.

"Police officers," Lew Sackler announced and put a
hand on the pusher's shoulder.

"Hello, Paulie," Dixon said. "Let's see what you've
got in your pocket."

"Nothing. I haven't got anything."

Sackler started to read them their rights.

"Take your hands off me, pigs." The young pusher
squirmed. "You ain't got no right to touch me."

Paulie Kellen was concerned only with getting rid of
the junk.

His teammates, lined up to get on the bus, became
aware that Paulie was in trouble.

"Police." Dixon identified himself and Sackler. "Get
on the bus."

"What's going on, Officer?" the driver asked

"Police business," Dixon replied. "Load your kids and
get out of here."

A crowd began to gather.

"Stand back," Sackler ordered as he pulled out the
cuffs and put them on his prisoner.

"We didn't do nuthin'," the dealer appealed to the
crowd. "They jumped us for no reason. I swear."

A murmur, low and growing ugly, swelled and the
crowd closed in. Sackler exchanged a nervous glance with
his partner. He didn't want to pull his gun, not even for

show. By unspoken consent, they began to edge toward their parked car, pulling the two boys along. Paulie Kellen was still trying to figure out how to get rid of the incriminating evidence in his pocket. The pusher continued to work the crowd.

"You gonna let them take us? You gonna just let them take us off the street without a warrant or nuthin'? Come on, help us out here. Come on!"

"Pigs!" a man yelled from the rear.

Somebody threw a rock.

The detectives ducked and it missed them both. It was followed by a scatter shot of gravel, which also fell harmlessly. But there was street work in progress and a pile of material was available to the crowd. Seeing that, Sackler and Dixon turned their backs and, pushing the boys in front of them, made it to their car.

The crowd followed. Fortunately, the parking space wasn't large enough for them to surround the car. However, by lining up along the sides, they could rock it. Dixon turned on the ignition. It caught promptly. He stepped on the gas and edged forward—he didn't want to run anybody down. That's all they needed at this point. Nor, fortunately, was the crowd interested in getting run down.

So they escaped.

As it turned out, Alfonso Martín, the pusher, was younger than he looked and younger than his customer. Not a big surprise to the detectives. For some years the users had been getting younger. Shockingly so. And lately, so had their neighborhood connection. It was standard practice for children to be used as couriers and bag men. If apprehended, they went before family court and, as juveniles, their sentence was light. That worked so well that the children had been promoted to pushing.

Alfonso Martín was only thirteen, but he was already a veteran of police interrogations. Since he was a juvenile,

Sackler and Dixon didn't have access to his record, but it was obvious from the way he handled himself that he had been arrested before. A body search turned up two hundred and fifty dollars in grubby bills. No drugs. He had managed, somehow, to get rid of them.

"Where did you get this money?" Sackler asked.

The boy shrugged. After giving his name and address, he hadn't spoken a word. And wouldn't, Sackler thought but went on asking anyway.

"How long has Paulie Kellen been buying from you?" Silence.

"Who else on the team has been buying from you?" Silence.

"How long have you been dealing from in front of the dance school? What made you pick that location?"

Alfonso Martín knew that his mother, accompanied by a lawyer provided by his boss, would show up and get him out. And it would be fast. He would continue to get that protection and prompt assistance till he was sixteen. Then the mob would drop him and he'd have to fend for himself. It didn't worry him. At his age, three years was a long, long time. By then Alfonso expected he would have a lot of money, more money than these cops who were leaning on him could make in a lifetime. It made it very easy to stonewall.

Sackler and Dixon went through the motions. When Mrs. Martín and the lawyer arrived, they had to let Alfonso go. They didn't bother to try to make a deal in exchange for information. The law had already made the child a better deal than they possibly could.

Paulie Kellen's situation was different. At sixteen, the law considered him an adult. His parents were upper middle class. He had all the advantages. He was superior to everybody in that place, he reminded himself as he waited in the holding cell. But he had never seen, much less been in, such a place and he was shaken.

So they let him wait till they were finished with Martín. Then they took him into an interrogation room. After eliciting his name, address, and age, they got down to it. Sackler started.

"How long have you been doing drugs, Paulie?"

The youngster held himself very straight, his blue eyes steady. "I don't do drugs, Detective," he replied. "Oh, I might snort a line every now and then." He shrugged, giving it no more importance than, say, a social drink.

These days everybody, including juveniles, knows you don't have to talk to the police without a lawyer present. Paulie certainly knew. He was showing off, Sackler concluded; maybe he thought that his willingness to answer questions indicated his innocence. "How often is *every now and then*? Every month? Every week? Every day? How many times a day?"

"Nothing like that. There's no pattern. I just do it . . . like . . . if I need a boost—before a game, say, or an exam."

"Sure." Sackler nodded. "I understand. And at parties, too, I suppose."

"Yes, at parties. Like everybody else."

Dixon took his turn.

"And how long has this been going on? Months? Longer?"

"I guess . . . longer."

"Which drug do you prefer? What gives you the best high?"

"I don't have a preference."

Dixon nodded sagely. "Whatever's available. I see. Who else on the team uses?"

Paulie flushed to the roots of his blond hair.

"How long have you been buying from Alfonso?"

No reply to that, either, not that one had been expected.

"Drugs cost money." Sackler picked up. They would now be throwing questions back and forth. "Where did you get the money?"

"I have an allowance."

"It must be pretty generous. Do your parents know what you're spending it on?"

Realizing that he'd said too much, Paulie Kellen turned away and refused to meet Sackler's eyes.

Dixon became sympathetic. "You've been caught with a large amount of drugs in your possession. That's serious trouble, Paulie. If you help us and give us the information we need, it will go easier for you."

"I'm not an informant," Kellen replied haughtily.

"You're protecting your friends. That's very nice. But will they protect you?" Sackler asked. "How about your parents? What are they going to say when they find out?"

That got to him. Paulie now raised his eyes and met Sackler's. "Do you have to tell them?"

A typical reaction that indicated lack of communication between parents and their children, Lew thought. He had no children, nor did he come from a large family, yet it saddened him. "Even if we wanted to, I don't see how we could keep it from them. They've been notified of your arrest and they're on their way over."

The last trace of color drained out of the teenager's face, along with the last bit of hope. He no longer held his head high as he was led back to the holding cell to await his parents' arrival.

Two hours after Paulie Kellen had been taken into custody, the Kellens finally arrived. It had taken a series of phone calls to locate them: Elizabeth Kellen at her bridge club and Paul Kellen, Sr., at a board meeting where he had left strict instructions that he wasn't to be disturbed. They came trembling from shock, indignation, anger. They came unaccompanied by legal counsel. They treated their child's arrest as an overreaction on the part of the police.

"Paulie's not an addict, Detectives," Kellen, Sr., insisted. "Nowadays all young people experiment with drugs. They're curious, that's all." He spoke with the broad New England *A*. Everything about him, his dress and manner, proclaimed privilege. However, the truth was that Paul Kellen, Sr., had not inherited his money and position; he had earned it by dint of hard work and shrewd manipulation. Kellen had profited by inside knowledge both for the benefit of his firm, Kellen, Schuman, and Forbes, and for himself personally. He liked to say that he was sometimes a bear, sometimes a bull, but never a pig. He kept his personal trading at a relatively modest level, and so far the Securities and Exchange Commission hadn't considered him worth bothering with.

"Drugs are certainly a blight on our society," Kellen continued. "Unfortunately, experimenting with them is a part of growing up. Almost a rite of passage. I'm not excusing Paulie, but you're putting him in the same category as the poor unfortunates who go out of control."

Control was this man's guiding doctrine, Sackler thought, and the son modeled himself on the father.

Dixon was grim. "Are you saying, sir, that you knew your son was doing drugs?"

"All right, yes, I did find out. And I had a talk with him about it. He said he'd only sampled a little cocaine. He said he didn't get anything out of it and he promised me he wouldn't do it anymore."

"And you believed him."

Kellen looked first at Dixon, then at Sackler. "Certainly."

"And how long ago did this little talk with your son take place?" Dixon wanted to know.

Kellen and his wife exchanged glances. "It was about a year ago."

She took the cue. "That's right, just about a year. It was spring. Paulie was on the basketball team, a star, and the play-offs were in full swing. The team was doing very well. They had a chance at the title. But Paulie was missing practice. The coach, Buzz Grogan, called..." She faltered.

Whereas her husband had worked hard to achieve money and privilege, Elizabeth Ward Kellen had been born into it. She gave the impression of statuesque beauty, but, in fact, she was too tall, her frame too bony, her New England accent, which Kellen copied, too broad. But in his view, her faults were the marks of breeding. He cherished and respected her, but there were times when she needed guidance.

He stepped in to help her now. "Once we were alerted to the situation, we put a stop to it."

"How did you do that?"

"As I said, I had a talk with the boy. Then I cut off his allowance."

"And that did it?" Dixon asked.

"Of course."

It would be the first time a kid who was hooked got turned off that easily, Dixon thought. "And that was a year ago and he's been clean since?"

"Yes."

"He had no other way to get money?"

Her husband was about to reply, but Elizabeth Kellen could no longer contain herself. "He took things."

"Elizabeth..." Kellen warned, glaring at her.

She was torn. How best could she protect her son—by continuing to hide the shame or by telling the truth? "We noticed some petty pilfering around the house and thought it was the servants. We had some new, part-time help. We decided not to say anything to them; it might have gotten very ugly. We just let them go quietly. But the thefts continued."

Classic, Sackler thought. First, the kids stole from home. It was easy, and their parents didn't want to believe it was happening. They ignored it as long as they could. "How did you find out?"

"We searched his room," Kellen admitted. Being forced to invade his son's privacy seemed to upset him more than the boy's addiction and thievery.

"And you found...?"

"We found the pawn tickets."

"We sent him away," Elizabeth Kellen blurted out. "We told our friends it was summer camp, but it was one of those detoxification places." She sighed, relieved to have set down the burden of silence. "When he came back he was... recovered. All the things he'd taken, we had redeemed. We put them out again and he never touched them. Not one. So that's how we know that he's not doing it, any of it, anymore."

She finished on a rising note. She wanted the detectives to believe. More than that, she wanted to believe herself.

"If Paulie's father didn't restore his allowance and he wasn't stealing from home, then where was he getting the money to support his habit?" Gwenn asked.

She had met Lew for a late dinner at a trattoria in her neighborhood. They'd finished the tricolor salad and were working on the linguini al pomodoro accompanied by a full-bodied Bardolino.

"Hopefully we'll find out tomorrow when we search his house."

"Tomorrow?" Gwenn twirled the pasta into a delicious mouthful.

"We can't just walk in and start opening closets and rummaging through drawers, you know. We need a warrant."

Though her mouth was full, Gwenn managed to indicate her disapproval.

Which Lew interpreted. "It's not urgent enough to disturb a judge in his home or to intrude on his evening out. Tomorrow will be time enough."

She swallowed, cleared her throat with the wine. "I hope so."

"Come on, Gwenn. Don't make a crisis out of it. We'll get a warrant first thing in the morning."

They were sitting side by side on a banquette. She turned so that she could look directly at him. "You expect the boy to keep the evidence waiting for you?"

"We let him go home with his parents, so he thinks he's safe. We confiscated the junk he had on him; he's not going to flush whatever else he's got down the toilet. No way. He's an arrogant kid."

"What about the parents? They might go through his things just to make sure."

Lew shook his head. "They don't want to know."

Gwenn nodded and went back to the linguini.

So did Sackler. After a few mouthfuls, he put the fork down. "If you've got something specific in mind, I'd appreciate hearing about it."

"Just a hunch. Still nebulous."

They resumed eating and by common consent there was no more discussion of the case. Finally, both plates were clean.

The waiter appeared. "Dessert?"

Gwenn shook her head. "Just a large decaf."

"Same for me," Lew told the waiter.

With a sigh of satisfaction, they leaned back against the banquette. It was a sign of appreciation for a good meal and the signal to talk about all the things that had been on their minds while they ate.

"So, if his allowance hasn't been restored and he hasn't been stealing from home, where has Paulie been getting drug money?" Gwenn picked up where they'd left off.

"Stealing from somewhere else."

"From the houses of his friends, maybe? Breaking in when he thought nobody was home?"

Remarkable how well in tune they were, Lew thought. They could analyze privately and, without explaining the process, reach the same conclusion. They had so much in common: not only were they in the same business, but they liked the same food, music, sports. She was a beautiful swimmer. He had an image of her lithe, strong body cutting through the water, arms reaching out, legs flutter-kicking in perfect form. She wasn't that good on a tennis court, but she attacked enthusiastically and laughed when she missed, a rare reaction among tennis players. Still, they hadn't yet made love. She'd made it clear at the start that she wasn't ready. He had at the time taken that as an indication that the relationship wasn't going anywhere.

He'd stopped calling, but he couldn't forget Gwenn Ramadge. Odd things reminded him of her. An ad for suntan oil brought to mind Gwenn sunburned and cheerful, much prettier than the girl on the billboard. A couple of times he'd thought he saw her driving the car she'd bought recently and of which she was so proud. He'd maneuvered his way through traffic, causing other drivers to throw on their brakes and blow their horns, only to discover when he pulled up alongside that it wasn't Gwenn after all. Obviously, the attraction was stronger than he'd realized. It was worth exploring. He called. He didn't offer an explanation for the interval of silence. She didn't ask for one. They had simply started seeing each other again.

He hadn't pressured her. He'd surprised himself on that. A couple of weeks ago on the way over to her place to pick her up for dinner and a movie, Lew stopped and

bought a small bouquet of spring flowers from a sidewalk
vendor. Flowers in hand, he'd felt suddenly like an ardent
swain on his way to propose. It frightened the hell out
of him. He'd almost stopped at a corner phone booth to
call and break the date.

Almost. He realized the idea of marriage had been
lurking at the back of his mind and that he was getting
used to it.

Since his mother's death, his father had suffered two
heart attacks. Lew had no brothers or sisters. Could it
be he now felt the shadow of his own mortality, the
need to propagate and carry on the name? Marriage
to the right woman might not be so bad. It might even
be good.

He took Gwenn's hand, raised it to his lips, turned it
over, and kissed her palm.

She was touched by the tenderness. It also made her
nervous. She didn't want him to make a declaration, not
yet.

"We'd better be sure to be at the Kellen house real
early tomorrow," she said.

That snapped him out of his daydreams. "We? What
makes you think you're coming?"

"Why not?"

"Because you're not a cop and you're not on the case,
that's why not."

"I'm not going to take part in the toss, for heaven's
sake."

"That's right, you're not."

"I'm not going to get in the way. You won't even know
I'm there."

"How am I going to justify your presence?"

"You don't have to. You're going in with a warrant
in your hand and a team behind you. You won't need
to explain to the Kellens."

"It's not the Kellens I'm thinking about. It's Sergeant Dixon. What am I going to say to him?"

"Tell him I'm there because of the possible connection, no, make it the probable connection to the Trent case." Her eyes held his. "It makes sense, doesn't it? I'm sure Ray will think so."

Chapter _____
_____ TEN

Getting a search warrant was not always easy and never automatic. The officer seeking the warrant had to find a judge willing to listen. Then he had to convince the judge there was *probable cause*. There were judges who had been sympathetic to Lew Sackler in the past, but waking one at seven in the morning was not likely to help his argument and expedite the process, which, on occasion, could take days. The Honorable Claude Merano finally agreed to issue the warrant to search the Kellen house and grounds for drugs and stolen goods.

That was well past ten A.M. Lew thought he had done well, indeed.

Having anticipated delay, it had been arranged that Ray Dixon would get to the Kellen place early and keep watch. He had just stationed himself in his car across the street when Gwenn, in hers, turned the corner. Dixon scowled. He had nothing against private eyes. They were competent to handle certain cases—divorces, corporate and white-collar crimes. They could be helpful where specialized knowledge of financial matters was required, or cases for which the police had no time. They had no business meddling in major thefts or embezzlements, and certainly not in homicides. They should never be present at a crime scene along with the police. Yet when Sackler told him that Gwenn Ramadge wanted to be present during the toss of the Kellen house, Dixon hadn't said a word one way or the other.

That didn't bother Lew. What did bother him was that Gwenn had predicted it. Coming along in her prized Volvo, Gwenn spotted Dixon right away. As she prepared to draw up alongside, Dixon waved her on.

She got the message, Dixon thought, watching as she drove past without any sign of recognition. From where he sat he had the entrance to the Kellens' house covered. One parked car was enough. He hoped she was smart enough to realize that and stay out of sight of the house. If she was really smart, she'd park around the corner and keep an eye on the Kellens' back door.

Nobody was going to try to sneak out, Gwenn thought as she took up the position Ray so obviously wanted her to. Why should they? The family could afford to behave normally. Kellen, Sr., would go to his office. Paul, Jr., would go to school. Mrs. Elizabeth Kellen wouldn't leave till much later. Gwenn hadn't had the chance to get any background on her, but Marge, who read the society and gossip columns avidly, said she was very social. Her first obligation of the day was likely to be a luncheon. Gwenn hoped she had nothing on earlier. She wanted Mrs. Kellen to be present when Lew showed up with the search warrant. Her reaction was what Gwenn had come to observe.

Lew Sackler, when he finally showed up, parked directly in front of the Kellen house and waited for Dixon to get out of his car and join him. Together they went to the front door, rang the bell, and moments later were admitted. Gwenn waited a full five minutes before following on foot. The timing was good, she thought. Mrs. Kellen would be too upset over the search warrant to care who

Gwenn was to question her presence. Gwenn had to ring twice before the maid opened the door.

The lady of the house appeared to be standing her ground. She spoke on the hall telephone while the two detectives waited. Gwenn couldn't hear what Mrs. Kellen was saying, but after only a short exchange she held the receiver out to Dixon.

Elizabeth Kellen wore a suit of dusky rose silk with a long sarong skirt, accessorized with several gold chains and large hoop earrings. All good eighteen-carat pieces, Gwenn thought, watching for any indication of nerves— a tremor of the hand, a twitch at the corner of the eye. Nothing. Instead, Mrs. Kellen, in handing over the telephone, acted as though she were bestowing a privilege on the detective.

Ray took it, listened, and then replied, "If you wish to come home with your lawyer, of course you have every right to do so, Mr. Kellen. We have a proper and legal warrant enabling us to conduct a search of these premises and we can't wait. But we'll probably still be here when you arrive." Politely, he handed the phone back to Mrs. Kellen. He waited till she hung up, then introduced Gwenn.

"This is Miss Ramadge. She'll be assisting us."

Elizabeth Kellen nodded without interest.

"To start with, we'll be taking a general look around. We'll try to cause as little disturbance as possible."

She was not reassured.

They started with the living room. It was furnished in solid mahogany, traditional and not particularly distinguished. What was most impressive was the number and quality of the accessories—sterling silver boxes, fluted crystal bowls, engraved trays, tiny enamel pill boxes. A full silver tea set, antique, probably Regency, was set on the cocktail table in front of the fireplace. In a vitrine on one side, a collection of Staffordshire birds was on display; in the vitrine on the other side, Victorian miniatures painted on ivory. It was certainly an accumulation of generations, Gwenn thought as she moved across the hall into the dining room to admire more silver and china. So many things, she thought. If something was missing, it was not likely to be noticed. Elizabeth Kellen's account of Paulie's thefts gained credibility.

In the library, they discovered the usual wall safe behind the usual oil painting—this one depicted a frigate in full sail.

"Would you look inside, please, and see if anything's missing?" Dixon asked Mrs. Kellen politely.

"We don't keep much here," she replied. "Cash for emergencies, certain documents, mostly to protect them from fire."

Everybody who had these safes said the same thing, Dixon thought. He wondered why they bothered to install them. "Still, if you'd take a look . . ."

Without further objection, Elizabeth Kellen stepped forward. She dialed expertly, swung the safe door open, then stood aside for Dixon to look. The contents appeared to be as she'd stated.

"How about jewelry?" he asked.

"That's upstairs in my bedroom."

She led the way. In the dressing room there was a vanity. She opened one of the drawers to reveal a pair of blue quilted satin trays. The contents were carelessly jumbled together: ropes of pearls, more gold chains, a string of dark red corals, all in a heap like cheap costume jewelry. But it was real, Gwenn was certain, when it came her turn to look. A square-cut emerald brooch, the stone about fifteen carats and adorned with rubies and diamonds, stood out from the rest.

"You have some beautiful pieces, Mrs. Kellen."

"Thank you. Most of them are inherited."

"And so doubly valuable. Aren't you nervous to have them lying around like this?"

She shrugged. "If a thief broke in, the first place he'd look would be the safe."

"I suppose so," Gwenn replied. "Which would you say was the most valuable?" She lifted the tray with the emerald brooch out of the drawer and held it in front of Mrs. Kellen.

"Prices fluctuate." Her voice quavered. She swallowed. "Sometimes diamonds are most in demand. Other times it can be rubies or sapphires. Selling, of course, is different from buying. You never get full value selling."

"Still, jewelry is a good investment," Gwenn observed. "One from which you can get some pleasure at the same time." She indicated the gold chains Mrs. Kellen was wearing.

"I'm going to a luncheon," she explained, her long aristocratic fingers barely touching the necklaces. "Otherwise, I seldom use any of my good pieces. To tell you the truth, I'm afraid for strangers to know I have such things." She took the tray from Gwenn, returned it to its place in the drawer, and shut it firmly. "Is there anything else you want to see?"

Gwenn looked to Dixon and to Lew.

"Your son's room," Dixon said.

She pointed. "On the third floor. He used to be just down the hall, but he got a stereo system. We couldn't take it." She smiled.

She was feeling easier, Gwenn thought.

"I know what you mean." Dixon smiled back.

"Unless you need me, I'll wait in the library."

As she started down, they started up.

Gwenn and Ray exchanged a look. Lew caught it and frowned, but he said nothing till they were on the third floor and well out of possible earshot.

"What's going on? Did I miss something?"

"You noticed she was relieved after she looked at the jewel tray?" Gwenn asked.

"Sure. So?"

"At first, she didn't want to look. I had to put the tray right in front of her. She didn't want to look because she was afraid something might be missing. She was afraid her son had started stealing again, but she didn't want to face up to that."

"When you forced her to look and she saw nothing was missing after all, she was relieved. She figures her son is in the clear," Lew concluded.

Gwenn sighed. "It would have been better if he'd gone back to stealing from home. Then he wouldn't have needed to break in to the Trent house."

"That's guesswork," Dixon told her.

"I prefer to call it a hunch."

"First you attribute a reaction to the woman, then you interpret it to suit yourself."

"That's not so!" Her green eyes flashed.

They glared at each other.

Lew intervened. "Woman's intuition, Ray. Gwenn's very strong on it, believe me."

"You can't build a case on intuition."

Why was he so touchy? Gwenn wondered. She looked to Lew, but he shrugged. Without further discussion, they entered Paulie Kellen's room.

It was modern, functional, a direct opposite to the traditional style of the rest of the house. It had a study area, an entertainment space. There were two beds, bunk style. It had the touch of a professional decorator. The parents had spared no expense. A casual look around wouldn't be sufficient here, Gwenn thought, particularly as they didn't know what they were looking for. So they divided the job. Sackler took the electronics, Dixon the desk and book shelves. That left the closet and bureau for her.

Gwenn had a teenage cousin and he was not noted for neatness. Few teenagers were. Paulie Kellen appeared to be the exception, she thought as she went through his wardrobe. Suits were at one end of the closet, slacks and jackets next, then jeans and sweats. His basketball uniform was probably in his school gym locker. She paid particular attention to the jeans and sweats. They were freshly laundered.

Next, she examined the contents of the bureau. Again, she was impressed by the orderliness. Shorts, T-shirts, handkerchiefs, socks, all in neat stacks. His mother or the maid was responsible, of course, Gwenn thought; one or the other policed the room. That surely limited his privacy. As she stood staring at the row of undershirts, Dixon came up to her.

"What?"

"I'm not sure. I think . . . I'm getting a picture." She went over to the bathroom. After a moment's hesitation at the threshold, she went to the hamper. She tossed out all the dirty clothes. When it was empty, she tilted it. "Let's take a look in the light," she said. The hamper was of white wicker; the stain was easy to see.

"His or the victim's?" Lew wondered aloud.

"I don't think Douglas Trent had a chance to injure his attackers. As far as we know, all the blood shed that night was Trent's. Some of it had to get on the perps."

Now both men saw where she was headed. In an effort to spare her, Dixon picked up.

"Kellen had no idea there would be so much blood. He was covered with it and had to stop the beating. But Trent wasn't dead."

Gwenn felt her stomach begin to churn. She turned aside.

"That's enough," Lew murmured to his partner.

Gwenn was pale, her lips pinched. She closed her eyes,

but the image remained vividly before her. It was ugly. Sickening.

"So he stripped down to his shorts and finished the job," she said. How could a boy do such a thing? she wondered. And because Kellen was so young her revulsion turned into sadness. "Then he went into the bathroom and took a shower."

"Gwenn, honey, don't say any more," Lew soothed.

"I need to get this out."

"We get the picture."

"I need to get it out," she insisted. "When Paulie finally got home, he discovered he wasn't completely clean. The shorts he'd kept on during the beating and in the shower still had blood on them." Once again she had to swallow back the acid bile. "So he stuffed them in this hamper where they lay till he had a chance to run them through the machine. They were damp and they left a stain."

She hadn't personally viewed the scene, Dixon thought, yet her reconstruction fitted as though she had. "That's good work, Gwenn. Very good."

The search resumed in grim silence.

It didn't take long for Lew to find the drug paraphernalia and a small amount of crack taped to the backs of the VCR and the CD rack.

"So he was running low," Lew remarked. "What we need to know is where he got the money for yesterday's buy and the buys he must have been making since he got out of detox. If he's been stealing again, his mother knows who his fence is—she said they'd redeemed all the stuff he took a year ago."

Gwenn shook her head. "She's not likely to tell us."

"He's not likely to have gone back to the same guy." Dixon shrugged.

* * *

It was Ray Dixon's opinion that you should always try the logical and easy way first. So he looked in the Yellow Pages under Pawnbrokers, which was probably what Paulie Kellen had done. Dixon was confronted by three pages of listings, which he then narrowed down according to location, picking as a starter the one nearest the high school.

Mel Wallach's was in Jamaica, Queens, under the El in an area seemingly undergoing urban renewal. Rows of tenements were boarded up. The road beds were rutted, there were pot holes everywhere, and the sidewalks were cracked. Just a block or so over toward Hillside Avenue, restored office buildings were already occupied. Fast food outlets—McDonald's, Roy Rogers, Nathan's— were doing good business, their presence attesting to their confidence in the reclamation of the neighborhood.

Mel had cast his lot with them. He'd modernized inside and out. The sign over the redesigned facade proclaimed: WALLACH LOAN ASSOCIATION. The traditional three balls were painted discreetly in the lower right-hand corner of the door. A gauzy curtain was drawn across the plate-glass window. Dixon rang the bell and they were buzzed in.

Gwenn looked around: it was like no pawnshop she'd ever seen. Where was the merchandise? The jewelry, watches, furs, musical instruments, cameras, stereos, hi-fis, TVs, VCRs, and so on? The place was bare. Walls and floor were of simulated marble. There were three writing stands in the center and a double row of plastic chairs along the walls on both sides. Teller windows were set in the wall opposite the entrance. If anything, it looked like a small neighborhood bank.

There was no one to be seen. Only one teller's window was open. Dixon walked over and leaned on the sill, then located a buzzer and pressed it. A young woman, seated at a desk in the rear of a large office area, was working at a computer. She looked up briefly, then went on with what she was doing.

"Police," Dixon announced and held up his shield case.

At that she stopped and looked over. Shelly Frank was pretty, young, fresh. Her hair was a nice, natural brown, cut in a page-boy style. She wore a mid-calf shirtwaist dress and bobby socks. A schoolgirl, working after classes, he thought. Unusual to find someone like her in a place like this. Meanwhile, Shelly had taken a close look at his ID.

"What can I do for you, Sergeant Dixon?"

Smart, too, and with plenty of confidence. "I want to see your boss."

"I'll tell him." She disappeared behind a partition. It wasn't long before a door in the corner marked Private opened and Mel Wallach himself appeared.

"Sergeant Dixon?"

He was a short, pear-shaped man. He wore an expensive suit, but the double-breasted style only emphasized his shortcomings. The psychedelic reds and yellows of the hundred dollar tie called attention to his pitted, sallow complexion. The thin film of sweat was probably due to a glandular condition and not nerves, Gwenn decided; surely in his business a visit from the police was not unusual.

Dixon made the introductions. "This is Detective Sackler and Miss Ramadge, a private investigator."

Wallach didn't comment, but he took a longer look at Gwenn, then waved them all into his private office. It could have been the office of a bank president. Done in British Country House style, it had the required dark paneling and a collection of hunting prints massed over a leather couch. It lacked only an artificial fireplace. Who in the world had put it together for him? Gwenn wondered.

Wallach answered her unspoken question. "My young lady out front, Miss Frank, did the decorating. Turned out nice, don't you think?" He beamed.

"Oh, yes," she beamed back.

"Got everything wholesale. Saved us a ton of money."

"Must have."

"So." Wallach settled himself at the large, leather-topped desk. Getting down to business, he addressed himself to the ranking officer.

"What can I do for you, Sergeant?"

"We're interested to know if you hold any pledges for a Paul Kellen, Junior."

He answered automatically. "All transactions are confidential."

Dixon had an automatic answer. "Going through your books entry by entry would be tedious and time consuming. We're really not interested in anything or anyone other than Paulie Kellen and what he brought in and how much he got for it."

"I'm not a fence."

"Fine. But if we're forced to go through your books and we discover some irregularity, we wouldn't be able to ignore it."

"I try to make sure the goods I take in are legit. I make every effort. Occasionally, something slips by. Or maybe one of my appraisers goofs."

"These things happen," Dixon acknowledged. "We're interested only in your dealings with Paulie Kellen," he repeated.

The pawnbroker considered, then opened out his hands in a gesture of surrender. "Always glad to co-operate with the police," he declared, and with that took a key ring from his pocket. He selected a key and unlocked the bottom drawer of his desk. He brought out a gray, cloth-covered ledger, which he placed on the blotter pad.

"I don't trust computers. We do our bookkeeping the old-fashioned way."

Everybody smiled.

Wallach turned the pages. "Ah, yes. Here it is: Paul Kellen, Junior. June seventh. He redeemed a pledge in the amount of twenty-five hundred dollars."

The date was significant to the detectives and to Gwenn Ramadge: two days after the break-in and murder.

"Redeemed," Dixon repeated. "What was the item?"

"A brooch." Wallach read off the entry. "One 18-carat square antique pin holding one square emerald, excellent color with natural inclusions, weighing 9.000 carats approximately and surrounded by 20 European-cut diamonds, total diamond weight 1.60 carats approximately."

They had seen the item that morning in Elizabeth Kellen's blue satin quilted jewelry tray.

"Value?" Dixon asked.

"Depends on whether you're buying or selling. If buying, it depends where. Tiffany's, I'd say it would cost you eighteen thousand."

They were impressed.

"If you walked over a few blocks to the Jewelry Exchange on West Forty-seventh, figure twelve thousand. Here, I'd be lucky to get eight or nine."

"And Kellen redeemed it for twenty-five hundred?"

"Plus interest, within the legal limits."

"If he hadn't shown up to claim it, that would have left you with a very comfortable profit."

"There's nothing illegal in it, Sergeant."

"I didn't say there was. When was the object pawned?"

"September fifteenth."

Not long after his return from detox, Gwenn thought.

"Didn't you wonder where a kid like Kellen got such an expensive piece of jewelry?" Dixon continued.

"Sure I did and I asked him. He said the piece belonged to his mother. She needed the money but was too embarrassed to come in herself."

"You bought that? Without checking?"

"I checked the item against the stolen properties list. It wasn't on."

He referred to the list of stolen goods circulated by the police. The pawnbroker was supposed to make sure an item offered to him was not on it. If it was, he was obliged to make immediate notification. If he failed to do that, the item could be confiscated and he would lose the money he had paid out. In this instance, even if she was aware that her emerald was missing, Elizabeth Kellen was not likely to report it. So the emerald had not been on the list and Wallach was in the clear.

"What else has Kellen hocked?"

Wallach hesitated. For a moment, it seemed he'd refuse to say any more. His place was near the school and for years he'd been dealing with the kids. Small-time stuff, most of it hot, which meant constant harassment from the cops. It was part of the cost of doing business. He took it in stride, that is till Shelly came to work for him. In less than a week he'd decided to marry her. He hadn't told her yet. Redecorating the premises was to impress her. It was part of his plan to go legit. For her sake. But when Kellen had come in with the emerald, he couldn't resist.

"What else, Mr. Wallach?" Dixon pressed.

"Nothing."

"You're saying you'd never done business with him before?"

"That's right. Never."

Dixon looked hard at the pawnbroker. "You didn't expect he'd redeem the emerald, did you?"

"Okay, I didn't. The kid was hooked. I could see that. I figured any money he could get his hands on would go to support his habit." He shrugged. The emerald was to have been Shelly's engagement present. It wouldn't be easy to find a value like that again.

They stood on the sidewalk beside their cars waiting in silence till the El above them rumbled past and they could hear each other again.

"He never bothered to redeem the other things he stole from home," Lew pointed out. "Why now? Why the emerald?"

"He didn't want his mother to know he was back on drugs," Gwenn replied.

"Okay. So where did he get the twenty-five hundred?" Lew persisted.

"He only knew one way." It was Dixon's turn. "He went out and stole. He heard through the grapevine Douglas Trent was going to be away for a few days and he knew that on Wednesday Mrs. Trent would be at the studio till late. It seemed a good opportunity. He came prepared to blow the safe. That suggests that he had been in the house before or at least had inside information. There were two of them, don't forget."

"But they didn't take anything," Gwenn pointed out.

"According to Emma Trent."

"Why should she lie?" Gwenn's color rose as she defended her client. She bit her lip. She had reacted too quickly. Instinctively.

Dixon didn't press the advantage. "So we'll see what Paulie has to say about it." He opened the car door. "Let's go get him."

"You're going to the school?" Gwenn asked. "You're going to pick him up right out of the classroom?"

"Are you saying we should care about his feelings? We should worry about embarrassing and humiliating him?" Dixon countered.

She shook her head. Paulie Kellen had given up the

right to consideration a long time ago. She didn't suggest
accompanying the detectives. It would have been unsuitable; it was unnecessary, and she didn't want to be
present to witness the boy's shame, deserved or not. So
they parted, Gwenn heading to the city and her office,
Dixon and Sackler to the school at the top of the hill.

Gwenn Ramadge had had no wish to be present at the
bust, nor did she want to sit in on the subsequent interrogation, to watch a young man at the threshold of his
life, enslaved by drugs, lie and squirm. What disturbed
Gwenn most was that Paulie was not unique, that he was
only one of countless victims of moral corruption. Her
distress must have been evident when she walked into
her office, because Marge Pratt, who was on the verge
of delivering one of her lectures on being kept informed
of Gwenn's whereabouts, took one look and remained
silent. And Gwenn stopped to talk.
   "They're arresting Paulie Kellen." She needed to
unload.
   "For drug possession?"
   "Blood stains were found in his room. If the lab
matches them to Douglas Trent . . . it will be murder."
She didn't mention she was directly responsible for discovering the stains.
   "How terrible. Will they try him as an adult?"
   "He's sixteen," Gwenn said, and with a heavy sigh
passed through to her office.
   She spent what was left of the afternoon doing paper-
work, paying bills, balancing accounts, enjoying the fact
that she had enough of a balance not to worry about
having a check bounce. Her accounts were right up to
date, but she dragged out the job waiting for Lew's call.
Every time the phone rang, she was sure it was him. He
would call to tell her the results of the interrogation,
wouldn't he? When Paulie was picked up on the drug

buy, his parents hadn't shown up for a couple of hours, and then without a lawyer. Well, they knew better now, she reasoned. They would come quickly and with legal counsel who would immediately caution the young suspect not to answer questions. And there was nothing the police could do about that. So he would go from arraignment to the bail hearing, and then, very probably, home.

There really was nothing for Lew to call her about, Gwenn reasoned. But he could call and tell her that, couldn't he?

Gwenn sent Marge home at the usual time, though she'd offered to stay. She puttered around till eight. When she couldn't find another thing with which to occupy herself, she went home, too. She fixed herself a bowl of lentil soup and wheat thins, watched some television, and was in bed by ten-thirty. She was sleeping soundly when the phone rang.

She reached for it, automatically noting the digital display on her bedside clock: 2:11 A.M.

"Gwenn, it's me," Lew Sackler said. "Sorry to wake you, but I thought you'd want to know. The kid's lawyer got together with the DA and made a deal. He admits to the break-in but not the murder."

Gwenn's grip on the phone tightened.

"Kellen claims he was solicited by a buddy to go along. The buddy was the one who beat Douglas Trent and killed him. His name is Adam McClure. We'll be picking him up in the morning."

Chapter _____ _____ ELEVEN

Adam McClure felt himself nodding and jerked his head upright and opened his eyes. The auditorium was quiet, warmed by the afternoon sun streaking in through the tall windows. It was a study period, but most of the fifty or so students seated down front were sleeping, having mastered the art of doing so while sitting erect. The teacher, seated at the desk on the platform facing them, had mastered the art of spotting them, but pretended not to see. He had his own work to do—a stack of test papers to be corrected; doing them there was preferable to carting them home and working on his own time. Also, he avoided confrontation with students whenever possible.

Adam McClure hadn't slept for many nights. He was afraid to sleep. Afraid of the nightmares. No, they weren't nightmares; they were not products of his imagination, of an upset stomach or fever. What he saw when he fell asleep, no matter how briefly, were repetitions of reality. Repetitions of what had happened in the Trent house. He couldn't forget. It was replayed over and over on the screen of his mind. Off to the left Paulie Kellen was actually studying. The events of that terrible night seemed not to have had any effect on him. He followed his regular routine, even attended class at the Dance

Studio. Adam couldn't bring himself to do that. The day before, he'd called in sick.

Paulie warned him he was attracting attention.

Adam had transferred from a prestigious private school only that past semester. He wasn't accustomed to the much larger and diversified student body, the mixture of economic and ethnic backgrounds that comprised the big public school. It was a microcosm of the real world and that was precisely what Randolph McClure wanted his son to learn to deal with. Formerly small of stature, the fifteen-year-old boy had a severe case of acne, and was self-conscious on both counts. He was not only uncomfortable in his new environment but also physically intimidated. His new classmates immediately sensed his discomfort and seized on him as the butt of their jokes and the object of their pranks. Paulie Kellen had come to his aid. He'd done it not out of pity or concern for his safety, and not because he'd taken a liking to the younger boy. Paulie Kellen used Adam's plight as a chance to establish himself as someone to be respected, even feared.

He faced Adam McClure's tormentors and threatened to blow their heads off if they didn't leave him alone. And he had the means to do it—a Glock, 9-mm semiautomatic. Few cops were permitted to carry one of those.

Adam had no idea why, but suddenly he had a protector and he was grateful. He idolized Paulie. He did everything Paulie told him to do without question. Then, suddenly, almost overnight it seemed, Adam shot up to his full height, six foot nine. In that regard at least, Paulie's equal. But he wasn't used to it. He was awkward, didn't know what to do with his arms and legs, like a puppy. Suddenly, he was valuable to the basketball team. But inside his awesome frame, the frightened boy still lurked. He continued to look to Paulie like a big brother. He continued to do what Paulie told him. Except for this last time.

Paulie had reasoned, explained, cajoled, and finally overcome Adam's qualms.

It had turned out to be worse than Adam could possibly have imagined. When the explosive charge they set to blow the safe open went off, he had been excited, even exhilarated. When they started up the stairs to the second floor, his heart pounded as though it would burst through his chest. At that moment, one part of him wanted to turn and run; the other drew him inexorably upward. Paulie had been in the lead. When the moment came, though, he had stepped to one side and left Adam to strike the first blow. And Adam had done it. Using the new strength he didn't know he had, he'd raised the bat high and brought it down on Mr. Trent's head. The shock of impact traveled through the bat into his hands and made his forearms twitch. The victim's skull cracked.

The victim, blood and bone fragments streaming down over his face, tottered. But he didn't go down. As the boys watched in fascinated horror, he took a step toward them.

Adam remained frozen to the spot.

Trent tottered another step.

At that, Paulie delivered the next blow. That brought the blood spurting and Douglas Trent went down on his knees.

Paulie jumped to one side to avoid the river of blood. "Hit him!" he ordered. "Hit him!" he cried and started to take his clothes off.

Stunned though he was, Adam again obeyed. Then Paulie, stripped to his shorts, joined him, and the blood lust possessed them both. They went on swinging their bats long after Douglas Trent lay motionless at their feet, his face a barely recognizable pulp. Out of breath, exhausted, a measure of sanity returned. They saw that the blood was all over them. They were standing in it.

They wanted to get out of there, but they couldn't go in the street as they were. They needed to wash off the blood. It was easy for Paulie; he just turned on the shower and got under it. Adam was fully dressed. The best he could do was sponge off his clothes, but it didn't help much. And it was getting late. They might be discovered at any time.

They fled.

They fled along the shadowed streets like shadows themselves, each to his own house. Both were expert at getting in and out without their parents' knowing. That particular night Adam's father was at a meeting and the housekeeper had the night off. Safe in his own room, the first thing Adam McClure did was take off his clothes and run them through the washer. He had no fear of being discovered; his father seldom got back before midnight and the housekeeper spent her nights off at her sister's. He interrupted the cycle to add his sneakers and that was when he remembered the bats. They'd left them behind.

They were just ordinary bats, he reasoned. No way to identify to whom they belonged. He was too tired to worry. He put on his pajamas and crawled into bed. As soon as he closed his eyes, he saw it all again.

Eyes open, he lay rigid for what seemed like hours. A little short of one A.M., a taxi pulled up and he heard his father's voice: they owned a car but it was in the garage; his father seldom used it except on weekends. Adam listened while his father entered and locked up and went upstairs. Gradually the house fell silent.

Suddenly a shriek ripped the darkness. He sat bolt upright, shuddering, and waiting. But there was no other sound. He must have slept only to be awakened by his own terror.

Had anybody heard?

He listened for footsteps, but apparently his father had

not been disturbed. Nevertheless, Adam was afraid to let himself sleep again. At six A.M., with the day's first light, the birds that inhabited the holly bush outside his window began their morning chorus. At seven, Sara Polsak, the housekeeper, came home. Adam got up and went about his regular routine. He turned on the radio, but there was no mention of Douglas Trent's death. They must have found him by now, Adam thought, somebody must have found him.

He managed to eat his breakfast, though Mrs. Polsak asked him several times if he felt all right. By the time he left for school, there still had been no mention of Douglas Trent's death.

At school, he looked to Paulie, but his friend avoided him.

Sometime during the interminable morning, the news did break and was immediately circulated through the school. Because the crime had been committed within the area and because Mrs. Emma Trent had nearly the status of a regular classroom teacher, the story passed through the halls like wildfire. The police were saying it had been a burglary gone out of control. That's what Paulie had said they would think. Paulie was always right.

Nevertheless, he stayed on edge. Days passed, then a week, and every time the doorbell rang Adam McClure thought it was the police, but it never was. There was no reason for them to connect him or Paulie to the crime, he told himself, and he was beginning to believe it. If only he could get some sleep! Paulie offered him a couple of snorts, but he'd said no. Maybe he should try it? How much longer could he go on like this?

The door down front at the right of the stage opened and two men entered the auditorium. The sun in Adam's eyes temporarily blinded him. Holding one hand up as a shield, he saw them go up on stage. One of them took a paper out of his pocket and showed it to the teacher. The teacher consulted a seating chart, looked out over the somnolent students, and pointed. At Paulie.

Paulie was aware, but didn't move. Neither did Adam. He watched in horrid fascination as the two men went over to Paulie and stood on either side of him. They got him to his feet and put the handcuffs on. They murmured something to him, then they walked him out.

Gradually, a realization of what was happening pervaded the auditorium. A low murmur spread. The students watched but didn't move. Adam was frozen in his place as the cops took his friend away. He would be next. He sat there waiting for them to come back and get him. But it didn't happen. The bell rang, marking the end of the period.

The students jumped up, shouting to each other. They pushed into the hall to spread the word that Paulie Kellen had got busted. For the second time. Everybody knew he'd been taken in just a day ago for possession. What could it be for this time? More of the same?

After everybody was gone, Adam was still in his seat. It wasn't till the next group filed in that he got up and wandered away. But for a few stragglers, the halls were empty. What should he do? He was scheduled for English, but he didn't want to be where the police could find him. He wanted to leave, but for that you needed a special pass and he didn't have one. Maybe he should go to his regular class? If the police had intended to pick him up, they would have got him at the same time as Paulie, wouldn't they?

Okay, so he'd go to class. Then what? He was afraid to go home. Obviously, they didn't know about him, and Paulie wouldn't talk, never, not Paulie. But they had ways of getting information. Without realizing, Paulie might let something slip. Suppose he went home and they were there waiting for him?

English was his last class of the day. After that, the doors of the school would open wide and the students would spill out like released prisoners. He would wait and be among them, he decided. He still didn't know where he would go. Not home, at least not right away; he'd made up his mind to that. Yet when the time came, he found himself heading in that direction. He took the shortcut, walking along the shoulder of the Turnpike toward Queens Boulevard. There was no sidewalk for pedestrians and traffic was heavy. Drivers honked and some shouted at him. Adam was oblivious. He felt dizzy, started to weave, and fell right in front of a small Pontiac sedan.

The driver slammed on the brakes, just in time. The driver behind him also stopped in time.

God! The two of them got out and came running to Adam, who was getting up slowly and shaking his head.

"Are you all right?" the first motorist asked. Seeing that he was, relief turned to indignation. "You've got no business walking out here. You could have got yourself killed, you know that, kid?"

"For God's sake!" the second man scowled. "You could have got us all killed." He pointed to the line of cars stopped within inches. "You started a chain reaction."

When Randolph McClure finally got home from the meeting of The Civil War Historical Society, the house-keeper, Sara Polsak, was waiting for him.

"Adam isn't home yet, Mr. McClure."

He looked at his watch: five after eleven. Late for a school night. "Where is he?"

"I don't know. He didn't come home for dinner."

McClure frowned. "He didn't let you know?"

"No, sir."

"He's usually pretty good about that," McClure remarked, more to himself than to her; courtesy was one of the things he tried to instill in the boy.

"Maybe there was an accident." She was very worried.

"Oh, I don't think so. We would have been notified. Probably he went to a friend's house and just forgot to call."

The housekeeper was not reassured. "I've called around. He was at school, but nobody's seen him since."

"Of course he was at school," McClure snapped; his son was no truant.

"Should we notify the police?"

Randolph McClure hesitated. A widower for five years, he was very much aware of his responsibility as a single parent and believed he was fulfilling it. He provided a good home and a housekeeper to run it. A good-looking man, tall and rangy, though not as tall as his son anymore, McClure had considerable charm and many lady friends. Out of respect for his wife and to spare Adam's feelings for his mother, he had never brought any of them home. Adam responded by studying hard, getting good grades, and staying out of trouble. These days, with kids wild as they were, that was a lot and he ought to be grateful, McClure thought. The boy should be rewarded. They should spend more time together. Maybe this summer he'd take a house at the shore...

McClure sighed deeply, walked over to the hall telephone, and picked it up. "Just to make sure," he told Sara Polsak.

The desk sergeant, Alain Deveraux, got a dozen such calls a night from agitated parents, particularly at this season. "It's getting close to graduation. There are a lot of parties," he strove to placate McClure. "Kids tend to lose track of time. Give him a while longer. He'll turn up."

Parents reacted to this advice in various ways: they accepted the explanation because they wanted to believe their son or daughter was merely having an innocent good time; or they persisted and demanded police action because they knew something was wrong, because it wasn't the first time their child had turned up missing. Randolph McClure fell somewhere in between.

"My son is not graduating, Sergeant, and he doesn't party. He's a good boy and a good student. He doesn't do drugs. I'm afraid something's happened to him." As he strove to convince the officer, he convinced himself. "Please check your accident reports. Check the hospitals."

"Sure, Mr. McClure. It'll take a while."

"I'll be right here waiting for your call."

"Fine."

"Don't you want his description?" McClure asked as the sergeant was about to hang up.

"Right. Go ahead."

"He's six foot nine, thin, with brown hair and brown eyes." He looked to the housekeeper. "What was he wearing?"

"Jeans, a light blue Lacoste shirt, a tan windbreaker," she answered promptly.

He passed it on.

"Okay, sir." Once again Deveraux tried to hang up.

"Don't you want my telephone number?"

"You've already given it to me, sir."

"Oh, yes, that's right. Well, thank you." At last he put the phone down, but only because he didn't know what else to say. "They're going to check," he told Sara Polsak.

She nodded. "Shall I make some coffee?"

"Yes, coffee would be good. Then you go on to bed. There's no need for you to wait up."

"I wouldn't be able to sleep."

He didn't argue.

In fact, Randolph McClure had no idea how long it would take for the police to get back to him. He didn't have a high opinion of their efficiency. The inadequacies of the department, the lack of manpower and venality, were a constant litany of the media, so that what little confidence the public had was undermined. But where could he turn? McClure agonized. He assumed a cop at the precinct was sitting at a telephone and calling the various hospitals in the five boroughs to check the night's accident victims. Would he ask about Adam specifically? Give his description? That could take hours.

He sat for a while. Got up and paced for a while. He didn't attempt to converse with Sara Polsak, but he appreciated her presence. He was grateful she cared enough about his son to keep watch with him. He didn't try to read or turn on the television or the radio. He didn't want distraction. The hours passed with agonizing slowness and he believed that the more time that passed the greater were the chances that no real harm had come to Adam.

It was a little after three A.M. when the phone rang.

But it wasn't the police. It was a neighbor, David Karlsberg.

"Randolph? Sorry to disturb you, but I just got home and I notice fumes coming out from your garage. Are you sure you turned off the motor?"

He hadn't used the car.

A flash of precognition choked the words in his throat and froze him to the spot. Somehow, he managed to shake it off, put the phone down, and run. He went through the kitchen and out the back to the garage, which was a separate structure. The side door was always unlocked. He yanked it open and clouds of blue exhaust smoke billowed out. With a handkerchief over his mouth and nose, choking and gasping, he plunged inside. He could make out his son slumped across the front seat. His eyes were closed. At last, Adam had found sleep.

The doors of the car were locked. By the time McClure had his keys out and had opened the door on the driver's side, Sara Polsak had raised the automatic door at the front. Together, they dragged the boy out of the car, across the cement floor, and out into the fresh, clean air. Neither one knew CPR and by the time EMS arrived, called by their neighbor, it was too late.

Adam was dead. His son was dead.

McClure stood and stared at his inert form lying in the driveway where he and Sara Polsak had pulled him. If only he'd gone to look for Adam when Sara told him he hadn't come home, he might have detected the fumes and been in time to save his son. If only the police had responded to his complaint and come over, they would surely have noted the fumes while there was still time.

They were now here in full force, parked the length of the block and on both sides. There were two emergency vehicles, four blue and whites, and a couple of unmarked police cars. It wasn't much longer before somebody from the Medical Examiner's Office showed up and kneeled beside his son's body and made what seemed to Randolph McClure to be a very cursory examination. The morgue wagon arrived and the attendants made preparations to take Adam away.

"Why?" McClure cried out and stepped forward to block them. Up to now he had stood to one side and let these strangers take over. After they found the suicide note on the dashboard, the detectives had gone into his house and up to Adam's room. Sara Polsak had shown them the way; the father stayed with his son. When they returned they showed him some things—clothing, sneakers—that they wanted to take. They handed him a receipt with every item listed. He barely glanced at it. But when they moved to take Adam, McClure came out of his torpor.

"Why? Why do you have to take him? You know what happened. You know how he died. Isn't that enough?"

"It's the law, sir," Dixon informed him gently.

"But he left a note. What more do you want?"

"Things are not always what they seem," Dixon said. In fact, Adam McClure's final words were clear.

Chapter

TWELVE

The note was a bombshell.

"I don't understand," Randolph McClure said in a low monotone and shook his head.

While police investigators swarmed over the driveway and the yard, McClure remained fixed beside the body of his son.

"Besides explaining his reason for taking his own life, your son implicates two other people in his crime," Dixon explained. The note had been immediately placed in a glassine evidence envelope. Handling it by the corner, he edged it out so he could read it once more:

"It was worse than I had ever imagined. I know Mr. Trent mistreated Mrs. Trent. He abused her and he deserved to die, but I wish we had done it some other way. She said to make it look like a burglary and that's what we did, but it was terrible. I can't forget. I didn't want the money. I told Paulie to keep it himself, or give it back to her. I didn't want ever to see her again."

At the bottom, almost as an afterthought, the writing becoming uncertain as the gas took effect, he'd added, "I'm sorry, Dad. Forgive me."

McClure moaned.

"Do you know the Trents?" Dixon asked and returned the note to the envelope.

"They live in the Gardens. I've seen them at the Community House and at PTA meetings. That's all."

"Your son took dance classes with Mrs. Trent."

"Yes, along with the rest of his team."

"Did he enjoy the classes?"

"As far as I know."

"Did he like Mrs. Trent? Did he talk about her?"

"He didn't talk about her. What are you getting at?"

"Never mentioned her?"

"No."

"The letter suggests otherwise."

McClure gasped. "He's only a boy. Fifteen years old. She's a mature woman. Married. My God, what are you suggesting?"

"How about girl friends? Did Adam have a steady girl friend?"

"I just told you . . . he's only fifteen."

"They start a lot younger than that. Some of them are already parents at fifteen."

McClure flushed scarlet. "Not Adam."

"What do you think Adam meant when he said, 'I know Mr. Trent mistreated Mrs. Trent'? And the money, what money was he referring to?"

"I don't know. I have no idea."

"Had he asked you for money recently?"

"No."

"Did you notice anything different about Adam lately? Did he appear depressed? Preoccupied? Unhappy?"

"No. I don't think so. I don't see that much of him, of course. We have breakfast together, then I go to work and he goes to school. I'm not home for dinner as often as I'd like. If I am here, he has studying to do. He's a very good student. He takes his marks seriously." He paused. "My wife died five years ago. I do my best for the boy," he said, continuing to speak of his son in the present tense.

"Let him go, Mr. McClure," Dixon advised. "Let the boy go."

McClure covered his face.

Dixon signaled for the body to be carried out.

For the second time that night, Gwenn was awakened by the ringing of the telephone. Again, it was Lew. Dixon had called him with the news and he now passed it on. Then he waited for her to comment. For the moment, at least, she was too stunned.

"I'm sorry," he said finally. "I know you believed in Emma."

"Yes."

"She fooled a lot of people."

Gwenn didn't reply.

"Well, I have to go . . ."

"When are you picking her up?"

"We're on our way."

Gwenn didn't even think about going back to bed. She put on coffee and while it perked she dressed. By the time she'd pulled on jeans and a turtleneck pullover, run a comb through her hair, and slashed on lipstick, the coffee was ready. She gulped it down scalding hot, black, no sugar. She needed a jolt. She left without rinsing out the cup and saucer, a sure sign of strain.

Gwenn Ramadge arrived at the station house on Yellowstone Boulevard at six-forty and took a seat on a bench in the corridor. She didn't have long to wait. Ten minutes later, her client, flanked by Dixon and Sackler, arrived. She looked dazed, Gwenn thought, not surprising considering how she must have been awakened, ordered to dress, and taken into custody. She wore no makeup, and her long hair was carelessly tied back. Passing Gwenn, she looked straight at her but didn't appear to know her.

"Emma," Gwenn called out.

Emma Trent stopped. Her eyes focused. She nodded

in recognition. "I didn't put them up to it. I didn't pay
them to kill Douglas." Her eyes filled. "I swear." Then
they moved her along.

At least she understood the charge, Gwenn thought.
She hadn't come with the expectation of speaking privately with Emma. She had come so that Emma would
know someone was there for her...prepared to help.

It wasn't long before Emma Trent was brought out
again and under the same escort. This time she was
guided to the rear exit, so there was no possibility of
further exchange.

"Has she contacted her lawyer?" Gwenn asked the
desk sergeant. "Do you know who he is?"

He shrugged, but he did divulge that the attorney
would be meeting Emma at Central Booking.

Satisfied that there was no need for her to follow
through, Gwenn went home. She took a hot shower followed by a cold rinse. Tingling and finally fully awake,
she changed into something less casual—tailored slacks
and a soft silk blouse. Then she fixed herself some eggs
and Canadian bacon and sat down to enjoy them. She
listened to the radio while she ate.

News bulletins regarding the most recent development
in the Trent case were being carried and discussed all
over the dial. The crime was divided into two parts,
equally shocking. It was bad enough that two school boys
committed the murder; the cold-blooded brutality of it
added to the horror. Paul Kellen, Jr., taken into custody
just the day before, had told police that he was not the
instigator. It was his buddy, Adam, who had devised the
plan and recruited him. Kellen didn't say why he had
agreed to take part. His lawyer arrived at that moment
and ordered him to stop talking.

Before the police got around to picking up Adam
McClure, he was dead. He left a suicide note naming
Emma Trent. *She said to make it look like a burglary and*

that's what we did. Those were the words quoted again and again. That was the reason the boys used baseball bats and beat the victim with such ferocity.

The second aspect of the crime was even more terrible. A young woman married to a rich man at least twice her age who wanted to get rid of him and hired killers was not unheard of. But seeking out two young boys, students in her dance class, who were in a real sense entrusted to her care, was beyond what even a society inured to shock could tolerate.

The charge was solicitation of murder.

Emma Trent denied it. Then, following the advice of her lawyer, she too refused to say any more.

Gwenn turned off the radio.

She felt in limbo. Naturally, Emma Trent's lawyer would be charting her defense. Undoubtedly, he had his own investigators and wouldn't need or want Gwenn Ramadge on the case. Which was fine with Gwenn. She wasn't at all sure she wanted to stay on it. She had believed in Emma and felt a great deal of sympathy for her. But if Emma had incited those boys to murder, then she was a monster and a superb actress as well. Gwenn's instinct said she was neither, but it would take a lot more than instinct to prove it. Gwenn had gone to the station house that morning to show support for her client and help her if it was possible. She was no longer under obligation.

The predicted rain was coming down hard when she went out at eleven. She spent the next several hours at the main branch of the public library tracing the history of Triad Paper, with little result. It was a private company and not listed in the standard directories. It was not required to publish its officers or board of directors. She left for her office in mid-afternoon with little to show for her efforts.

Marge Pratt was on the telephone. Her eyes lit up

when she saw Gwenn. "She's just come in, ma'am. Just a minute, I'll put you through." She covered the mouthpiece with her hand. "It's her," she whispered.

Gwenn frowned. "Who?"

"Her." Marge hissed insistently. "Mrs. Trent, who else? She wants to talk to you."

"All right, put her on." Deliberately, she took time to collect herself, putting aside the dripping umbrella and hanging up the sodden raincoat, while Marge Pratt's exasperation grew. Finally, she picked up the extension in her office.

"Mrs. Trent? Where are you?"

"Home."

"I'm glad to hear that." She'd made bail fast, Gwenn thought.

"You advised me to get a good lawyer."

"Who did you get?"

"Amos Quilling."

A man not known for losing regardless of his client's innocence or guilt. He took on a client either because he could charge an astronomic fee or get the equal in publicity. "They don't come any better."

"But I need to talk to you," Emma Trent said. "Please. Would you come over? As soon as possible."

The rain had tapered to a fine spring mist. Everything was green in the Gardens. On Clinton Place the magnolias and cherry trees had blossomed and were dropping their petals, forming a soft pink carpet. As blue twilight faded into night, the lights in the houses started to come on. Yet Gwenn was not soothed. Instead, as she walked up the path to the Trent house, she had a sense of abandonment, of desolation. Only a few lights were on there. The last time, the place had been ablaze and full of activity, she recalled, waiting for the maid to let her in.

But it was Emma Trent who put on the porch light,

peered through the peep hole, and opened the door. Once Gwenn was inside, she turned the porch light off. In the hall, a single lamp glowed dimly.

"They're gone—Jonathan, Sheila, and the children," Emma told her. "He said he wouldn't stay under the same roof with me."

Her face was drawn and haggard. Dark shadows accentuated her large eyes, which kept darting from one place to another as though . . . as though she were looking for something or expecting someone? Gwenn wondered. Would that attitude count for or against her with a jury? Then she caught her breath, shocked at her assumption that Emma Trent would go to trial.

"Where did they go?"

"Home. To Toronto. They'll be back to testify against me. Jonathan made sure to tell me." She sighed. "I don't suppose I can blame him."

Gwenn didn't know what to say. While she tried to think of something, the phone rang. Emma Trent looked at it, and for a while Gwenn thought she wasn't going to answer. But she did.

"Hello?"

There was a tremor in her voice. She listened for a considerable period while the person at the other end talked on. At last, without a word on her part, Emma Trent hung up.

"That was the mother of one of my pupils. She's taking the child out of my school. She isn't the only one. I can't blame her, either, or any of them. Why should they give me the benefit of the doubt?"

Because they entertained no doubt, Gwenn thought. In their minds, Emma Trent had already been convicted.

"At least she didn't call me any filthy names," Emma Trent said as she led the way into the living room.

The drapes were drawn and, as in the hall, only a single shaded lamp was lit.

"Can I get you some coffee?"

"No, thanks."

Emma Trent took a deep breath. "I'd like you to continue your investigation."

Gwenn had her answer ready. "Your defense is in expert hands. Amos Quilling is far more experienced than I am. He not only knows what to look for, he has a large staff to do his research. I'm alone with only a secretary."

"Mr. Quilling doesn't care whether or not I'm guilty. He doesn't believe in me. If he gets me off, it will be on some legal technicality; that's his style. I want my reputation cleared. I don't want to go through life with people pointing fingers and whispering behind my back. You know my story," she pleaded. "You know I was suspected of killing my first husband. The police could never prove anything. They finally gave up, but the shadow continues to hang over me. I don't want that to happen again."

"It's not likely to," Gwenn replied. "Your first husband had a heart attack. You were out at the time. He couldn't get to his medication. It was impossible to prove you deliberately put it out of his reach. As I told you before, it's very difficult to prove a negative. In this case, you're facing a dying declaration. That's almost impossible to defend against."

"I didn't do it."

"If Adam McClure were alive, we might probe his motive, shake him, get him to retract . . . but he killed himself because of what he claims you paid him to do." Gwenn sighed heavily. "His suicide puts credibility and sympathy all on his side. We don't dare cast any aspersions on him."

"How about his friend, Paulie? He admits participating."

"That's right, he admits going along but sticks to his

story that Adam was the instigator. Paulie made a deal with the DA and turned Adam in."

"He's lying! I didn't hire anybody to kill Douglas. To start with, I didn't have any money."

Gwenn frowned at her. "What do you mean, you didn't have any money?"

"Just that. Douglas gave me enough to run the house. I had no money of my own. If I wanted to buy a new dress, I had to ask. If I wanted to get my hair done, I had to go to him."

"How about the dance studio?"

Emma Trent lowered her eyes. "Things haven't been going so well."

"I had the impression it was very successful."

"No." It seemed as though she would enlarge on the denial; instead she shifted to another defense. "Suppose Adam hadn't written that letter, there'd be nothing against me."

"But he did write it," Gwenn retorted, more sharply than she'd intended. "It's a powerful accusation. We must deal with it."

"How?" All of her desperation was in that one cry.

Gwenn opened her handbag and brought out a notebook. "Let's look at what Adam wrote: *I know that Mr. Trent mistreated Mrs. Trent and abused her and he deserved to die.* That's strong language and very damaging. It indicates your marriage was far from happy, as you originally presented it. If your husband was in fact abusing you, it gives you a powerful motive for having him killed."

Emma Trent bit her lip. "It's true," she admitted. "Douglas beat me and terrorized me and he'd been doing it for a long time."

It had been a test question, and if her client had persisted in her denial, Gwenn would have walked out. "How long?" she asked.

"It started about six months after we were married. He was very jealous. Little by little, he caused me to stop seeing my old friends, male or female. I didn't have any money of my own, so I couldn't go to lunch or anything like that. He dictated what I should wear, particularly when we went to any of his business affairs together. Once when I bought a dress for a particular dinner, he got the scissors and cut it up because he considered it inappropriate. He constantly criticized my behavior. He said I embarrassed him in front of his friends. He hit me."

"And this continued over a year and a half?"

"It got worse and worse."

"But nobody knew?"

"Mostly he made sure to hit me where it wouldn't show."

"Why did you put up with it? Why didn't you leave him?"

"I did. I tried. A couple of times. After a particularly bad beating, I waited till he was out of the house and then I sneaked away. But he always found me and came after me and told me how sorry he was. He said he loved me and he was jealous, that's all. He begged me to come back. He cried."

Classic pattern, Gwenn thought, and pitied Emma Trent.

"So I told him I was lonely at home alone all day. I was accustomed to being active. I needed something to do. I thought of starting a dance studio, and he agreed to let me do it."

Let me. It was not lost on Gwenn.

"He advanced the money for me to get started—to rent space, put in the equipment, get it decorated."

"And?"

The tears welled up in the amber eyes. "I guess he

expected it to fail. That would have robbed me of my last shred of self-confidence, that would have made me completely dependent on him."

"So it didn't fail?"

"From the first day the doors opened it was a success. There was a drain on the profits to pay off the start-up expenses, naturally, but I kept my head above water. What made me really happy was that the community accepted me. That's what I valued most.

"I think that's why Douglas changed his attitude. He started to complain that the studio took up too much of my time, that I was never home; I was never available to accompany him to business functions. Which wasn't true. I only missed one affair and I learned that very few of the wives had attended anyway. I cut out all evening classes but one so I could go out with him. I made myself available. Then he didn't want me."

"And all this time he was abusing you, and nobody knew. You didn't tell anybody."

"I was ashamed."

Yes, she could understand that, Gwenn thought. "How did Adam find out?"

Emma didn't answer.

"His letter suggests a close relationship between the two of you." Gwenn's eyes were fixed on her client; her tone warned she would not tolerate any more evasions. "You've got to be straight with me."

"The boy had a crush on me. I sensed it. It was an ordinary schoolboy crush. I knew that his mother had died not so long ago and I could see he was a lonely child without many friends, and I felt sorry for him. I didn't encourage him, but I didn't rebuff him, either. I didn't want to hurt his feelings."

Constantly subjected to disapproval and antagonism as she'd been, she'd found some solace in the teenager's admiration, Gwenn thought. She repeated her question.

"How did Adam find out your husband was abusing you?"

"It was a Tuesday afternoon in early March when the team came for class. They'd all left and there were no other lessons scheduled, but I didn't go home. Douglas had said he'd be working late, so I decided to work late, too, mostly balancing my books and getting a start on my taxes. Actually, Douglas didn't approve of my work with the boys, and on the days they came he was particularly irritable."

"You were afraid to go home?"

"I was also afraid to be too late. If Douglas got home before me, that wouldn't be good, either. So, as I was about to close, there was a knock at the door. I don't know if you're familiar with the layout of the studio, but I'm on the second floor. There's a door on the street that opens to a private stair leading to the studio. The knock was at the upstairs door. I was surprised because I thought both doors were locked, and for anybody to come up I would have had to buzz them in from downstairs. The cleaning people had a key, but they weren't due till much later.

"I thought it might be an intruder and I was frightened. I had my hand on the phone to dial 911 as I called out, 'Who is it?' But even as I asked I knew the answer. It had to be Douglas. I wondered how he got a key—probably took mine off my ring and had it copied. He did things like that. So I figured he must have a key to the upstairs door, too. Why didn't he use it? Because I had the bolt in place, of course. So I got up and let him in.

" 'Well,' he said. 'Why aren't you home?'

" 'You said you'd be working late,' I answered.

" 'I rushed. I figured you'd be lonely. I thought you'd be waiting for me,' he said.

" 'I was just leaving,' I told him. 'I'll get my bag.'

" 'No, no. It's just as well I'm here. I've been meaning to talk to you. This is as good a time as any.'

"He started advancing toward me and I backed up till we were in a little room at the rear that I use as an office. He motioned for me to sit in my own chair at the desk. I didn't have any idea what he was up to. None. I was completely unprepared for what came next.

"He said he was not happy with our arrangement. He didn't want his wife working. It didn't look good. He wanted me to close the studio.

"I couldn't do it. I just couldn't. The studio was the one thing I cared about. It kept me alive. I told him no and then I braced myself for the first blow. Oh, he hit me all right, but not in the way I expected.

" 'You're not going to run it on my money,' he told me. 'I want my money back. All of it. Now.'

"I didn't have it. I'd recently put in a new sound system and upgraded the two locker and shower rooms. He knew that. I needed time.

"He wasn't interested. He didn't care.

" 'It wasn't a gift,' he said. 'It was a loan and now I'm calling it back.'

" 'I haven't got it,' I told him again.

"Then he hit me. He hit me hard, across the face. His ring cut my lip. That time I believe he wanted it to show. He wanted to shame me publicly. Anxious to convince him, I made a big mistake.

" 'I've got barely enough to cover rent and utilities for the next two months,' I told him, and showed him my checkbook.

"He snatched it out of my hands, tore out a check, and ordered me to draw out every penny.

"He hit me and hit me and hit me till I did it. I could barely scrawl my name, but I filled out the check and handed it to him. Then he wanted to know what cash I had on hand. I opened the drawer and he took the petty cash. He stuffed the bills into his pocket and stalked out.

"When I was sure he was gone, I sat down, put my head in my hands, and cried. I didn't hear the downstairs bell, I didn't hear the studio door open. I didn't hear anyone come in, but after a while I was aware of a presence. I looked up and saw Adam. I suppose he must have come in as Douglas was going out and found the upstairs door ajar. Anyway, there he was standing in front of my desk and gaping at me.

"When I looked up, he gasped. I suppose I looked pretty bad.

"'What happened? Can I get you something? A glass of water?'

"I was glad to have somebody there in case Douglas should decide to come back, though that wasn't likely. Usually, after such an incident, he'd go out... I don't know where. Not drinking, he wasn't much of a drinker. He'd be gone for hours. I'd lie in bed waiting with the door unlocked. When he got back, he'd try the door and then go to bed in the room down the hall."

Gwenn didn't say anything, but she thought plenty. Mental torture added to the physical.

"The boy was sympathetic and embarrassed at the same time," Emma Trent continued. "He didn't know what to do for me or how to console me. He went to the bathroom and soaked towels in cold water and helped me clean up. Then he pulled over a chair and sat beside me. After a while, he took my hand and held it." Her large, limpid eyes were full of tenderness. "At that moment, if he'd made the slightest overture—put his arm around me, brushed my cheek with his lips—no matter how tentative or awkward, I would have responded. But he sat there stiffly, blushing with desire and afraid to do anything about it. He looked so young. I couldn't... use him."

Chapter
THIRTEEN

"Why did Adam come back?" Gwenn asked. "You say his class was the last one of the day. You should have been gone."

"I never thought of that. I don't know why he came back. He never said and I never asked. I suppose he forgot something: his books, wallet, something in his locker."

She shrugged it off, but Gwenn considered it important. "You believe he passed your husband on the stairs?"

"Yes."

"You believe he recognized your husband?"

"From the way he acted, yes."

"So he must have met Mr. Trent at some time."

"The school held a recital at Christmas. Adam took part and Douglas attended."

Darkness had fallen and the rain stopped. The street lights were on, but they were dim and partly obscured by trees casting deep shadows. From time to time heavy gusts parted the drapes and the shadows reached into the room.

"The next time you saw Adam McClure, did you discuss the incident?"

"No. We were never alone together again."

Gwenn was thoughtful. "But Adam did continue to attend classes along with the rest of the team?"

There were beads of sweat across Emma's brow and upper lip. The room was hot and stuffy; Gwenn was sweating too. She was going to suggest turning on some more lights and letting in some air when, abruptly, Emma rose and strode to the window. But instead of parting the drapes, she drew them closer. After that, she turned on one more lamp.

"We were never alone together again," she reiterated.

Gwenn let it go. "After your husband cleaned out your checking account, how did you manage to stay in business?"

"I appealed to the landlord for a grace period on the rent. I told him I had some personal problems and I would pay up within three months. The space had been empty a long time and I suppose he didn't relish looking for another tenant. Also, he could see things were going well as far as attendance was concerned. Actually, he's a nice man and I think he wanted to help. He said not to worry. He said if I had a problem with other creditors, to refer them to him. I was concerned about the utilities, but I decided I would be able to pay those bills from the money that came in on a weekly basis and from individual lessons."

"Your husband didn't take that from you?"

"He never even talked about the money again. I kept expecting him to. It was like waiting for the other shoe to drop."

Or like leaving the bedroom door open, though terrified that he would come in. "Did you ever think of going to the police?"

"He would have killed me." It was a statement, flat, devoid of emotion.

There were plenty of cases in which a battered wife

had appealed to the court for an "order of protection," which had merely served to spur the husband to greater fury, driving him to show his contempt for the law by continuing to beat his wife till he killed her.

"Let's go back to Adam's note." Again, Gwenn read from her notebook: "*She said to make it look like a burglary.*"

"I never said any such thing," Emma Trent protested. "I never spoke to either of the boys about my private life. I never solicited them, or anybody else, to commit murder for me. Never."

Gwenn continued, still reading: "*I didn't want the money. I told Paulie to keep it for himself or give it back to her. I didn't want to see her ever again.*"

Emma Trent shook her head.

"Again, I remind you that we're faced with a dying declaration, which carries a great deal of weight."

"He lied. I don't know why, but he lied. You've got to believe me."

And to her own surprise, Gwenn did. Adam McClure's last words could not be discredited, but maybe they could be reinterpreted. *She said to make it look like a burglary.* Wouldn't it have been simpler and more direct to say: *She told me*, or *She told us* in the same way he had said regarding the money: *I told Paulie to keep it himself or give it back to her?*

"I didn't have any money," Emma Trent insisted. "I couldn't pay my rent. So where was I going to get money to pay off killers?"

Gwenn went on reading, "*I didn't want to see her ever again.*" Then she broke off. "But he did continue to see you after the murder, didn't he? He continued to attend classes."

"That's right."

"Presumably what he meant was that he didn't want to see you alone," Gwenn mused. "But he hadn't been seeing you alone—except on that one occasion."

The two women looked at each other, at last perceiving a narrow avenue of escape.

"He could have been talking about somebody else." Gwenn put the hope into words.

"Oh, yes! Oh, please, God!"

"But we need evidence that somebody else hired the boys. If we get it, we can counter the letter. As things stand now, the letter is damning."

"I understand," Emma Trent said, but the flame of hope would not be extinguished.

The two women walked together to the front door. Emma Trent put on the porch light and stepped outside with Gwenn. For a moment they stood together as though on a lighted stage, then Gwenn started down the steps. As she did so, a stone came hurtling out of the darkness past her and hit Emma on the left shoulder.

"Murderer!"

"Whore!"

"Get out. We don't want you here."

"Bitch! Get out, bitch."

Kids, Gwenn thought, peering into the darkness. In fact, a bunch of youngsters were congregated at the corner, seemingly too young for this kind of viciousness. She could see no adults among them, but she was more concerned with getting Emma back into the safety of the house than in trying to identify the culprits. She literally pulled her client back inside and slammed the door shut.

"Are you all right? Let me see your shoulder."

"I'm okay. It's just a bruise. Nothing serious."

"I take it this isn't the first time."

"It's the first time they've thrown anything."

"Well, we'll make sure it's the last."

"How?"

"Call the police."

"They won't do anything. What can they do?"

"Post a guard."

"They won't."

"Have you asked?"

She shook her head. "Why should they care about me?"

"It's their job to keep the peace," Gwenn replied and, green eyes flashing, headed for the telephone at the back. She dialed not 911 but the local precinct. "Detective Sackler, please."

Lew picked up promptly, which Gwenn indicated to Emma with an encouraging smile.

"It's me, Gwenn...Yes, I'm fine. Listen, I'm over here at Mrs. Trent's. We've got a bunch of kids throwing rocks and shouting nasty remarks...No, she's not hurt. Not this time. The stone glanced off her shoulder. Will you send somebody to stand guard?"

"Is this the first time?" Lew wanted to know.

"She's been harassed over the telephone and she's gotten hate mail."

"Is this the first overt act?"

"All right, yes, it's the first. But it's going to get worse. You know that. She's all alone in this big house..."

"How about her family?"

"They left, walked out. Come on, Lew, this is a dangerous situation here."

"All right, I'll talk to the lieutenant, but I doubt..."

"I can't believe you're making such a fuss about this. One squad car parked in front of the house, that's all it's going to take. You can spare one car, for heaven's sake."

"It's not up to me."

Gwenn groaned.

"All right, all right. I'll see what I can do."

"Don't bother. Forget it. I'll stay myself. As it happens, I've got my gun. We'll be okay."

Lew knew she didn't carry it regularly. She must have had a hunch she'd be needing it. "Okay, you've made your point. I'll take care of it."

"Thanks, Lew. I knew we could count on you." She gave Emma a thumbs-up. "Are you on your way?" she asked Sackler.

"Is it all right if I stop to pick up something to eat?"

"You bet. While you're at it, get a tuna on rye for me." She looked to her client. "The same for Mrs. Trent. We'll make the coffee."

"Will that be all?"

From where she stood, Gwenn could look out on the street. She lowered her voice to avoid alarming Emma. "No, you'd better get some backup. The crowd's getting bigger." She hung up and flashed a bright smile. "We're all set for tonight. Detective Sackler will stay with you."

"Thank you."

"No thanks necessary."

"He wouldn't be doing it but for you."

"Of course he would. It's his job." He *was* doing it for her, Gwenn thought, and probably on his own time. So they were okay for tonight, but what about tomorrow and the day after? She couldn't expect Lew to stand guard indefinitely. On the other hand, why anticipate tomorrow's problems?

"Come on," she said to Emma. "Let's get the coffee started."

By the time Lew Sackler arrived, three RMPs were lined up in front of the Trent house. It was more than enough. The neighborhood youngsters, not accustomed to confrontation with the police, dispersed at their first glimpse of the blue and whites.

After an informal meal of the sandwiches Lew had brought, the coffee the women brewed, and the rest of the chocolate cake left over by the Trent children, Gwenn went home. What she had learned that afternoon only added to the case against Emma Trent, yet Gwenn left still believing in her innocence.

Gwenn's best thinking was usually done stretched out on her living room couch, relaxing with her eyes closed, allowing her thoughts to drift. Tonight she remained tense and her mind refused to go beyond the ugly situation in which Emma Trent had been trapped. There could be no doubt that she had a powerful motive to kill her husband. In fact, her motive was now shown to be so strong as to surmount all others. In addition, the notion that she might have been responsible for her first husband's death, though not likely to be introduced as evidence, would cast an additional shadow. The only way to clear her was to find the real perp, the person who had hired the boys and paid them to kill Douglas Trent.

Paulie Kellen had not named her client, but by shifting the role of leader to his friend, Adam McClure, he implicated Emma. When he testified against Adam he would be implicating her. Once known, the gentle, bittersweet relationship between Emma and the younger boy would make the accusation all the more damning.

But if Emma was telling the truth, then Paulie was lying. Was he, not Adam, the instigator?

Gwenn was not an early riser, and when her phone rang at eight the next morning, she was still in bed.

"Good morning." Lew was cheery. "Sleep well?"

"As a matter of fact, yes, very well. How about you? Had a good night?"

"No, but everything's okay now."

It wasn't the answer she'd expected. "What happened?"

"More of the same," he told her. "Only this time it was adults, and not from the neighborhood, either. They were imported. They came in buses."

God! she thought. "So, what's the decision?"

"We're posting a couple of squad cars, probably through the weekend."

"She'll be a prisoner in her own house."

"But she'll be safe. That's what you wanted, isn't it?"

"Yes. But how about the Kellens? Anybody bother them? Anybody congregate in front of their house? Throw rocks at them?" she asked with a flare of indignation. "Why is everybody against Emma?"

"She's the outsider. The people here are basically decent. They can't bring themselves to admit evil in their midst. They don't want to face the fact that they allowed it to flourish. So they have to turn the blame on somebody else. They believe she corrupted the boys."

"And that takes the responsibility off them," Gwenn concluded sadly, and hung up.

What next? she wondered. Her leads had dried up. She had learned a fair amount about the suspects, but very little about the victim. So far, Maurice Jessup had been the only one disposed to discuss Douglas Trent. She decided to go back to him.

Jessup greeted her cordially. "Would you care for coffee?" he asked when she was seated.

"No, thanks. I know how busy you must be. I won't take up your time."

"I want to help."

"Thank you. As you know, I'm working for the widow, Emma Trent."

"The way things have devcloped, I can't see there's much you can do."

"I'm interested in the situation here at Triad, particularly the meeting Mr. Trent called for Thursday, June sixth. Have you any idea what he wanted to discuss?"

"None."

"According to his secretary, he was agitated. There are indications that he wasn't satisfied with the way the Toronto office was being run. He suspected irregularities. Do you know anything about that?"

"Not really. Jonathan, his son, was in charge. As a father, Douglas was supercritical. He demanded too much. At the same time, he pushed Jonathan ahead too fast. In spite of that, Jonathan managed to cope."

Pretty expert hedging, Gwenn thought. "Would you mind if I had one of my accountants take a look at the Triad books?"

He was not enthusiastic. "Your client has no shares in Triad," he reminded Gwenn. He was thoughtful, almost brooding. "You think Jonathan was embezzling and his father found out?"

"I'm floundering, Mr. Jessup," she admitted. "I'm looking for something and I don't know what."

"I understand." The set of his low-slung jaw eased. "As a matter of fact, accountants are going over the books now. We need to determine the company's worth for inheritance tax purposes and, of course, for the IRS. Your accountant can come in at any time."

"Thank you."

He waited politely. "Is there anything else?"

"Yes, Mr. Jessup, there is. When we talked the last time, you indicated that the marriage of Douglas and Emma Trent was a happy one."

"Yes. As far as I know."

"It now appears it was anything but. Mrs. Trent says he abused her. Repeatedly."

Jessup gasped. He seemed genuinely shocked. "I find that hard to believe. Douglas had a temper, but he usually held himself under control."

"She wouldn't lie about a thing like that."

"Hardly," Jessup agreed. "It doesn't help her cause."

She believed in Jessup's integrity. Still, taking a look at the books couldn't hurt. She'd send Al Benjamin over. If the books were cooked in any way, he'd spot it. Al didn't come cheap, but she didn't think Emma Trent would object to the cost.

Albert Thomas Benjamin was not one to waste either his time or his employer's money. For forty-five years he had been chief trouble shooter for LeGrange, Dorsett, one of the top accounting firms in the country. He was a wiry, gray man with a bulbous nose and dark, sparkling, penetrating eyes. Summer or winter, rain or shine, indoors and out, he wore the same green fedora with a feather in the band. Gwenn couldn't remember ever seeing him without it. He reminded her of a mischievous leprechaun. When the time had come for Al Benjamin to retire, he opened his own shop and thrived. The more complex the scam, the more devious the manipulation, the more he enjoyed uncovering it. He would present himself, smile, and rub his palms together, an indication, Gwenn had learned, that a juicy morsel was about to be set before her. On this occasion, as on many others, she pleaded urgency. He agreed to work through the weekend.

Lew would be on guard duty at the Trent house through the weekend.

Gwenn found herself with nothing to do.

Well, not exactly. There were plenty of jobs at home and in the office. She just wasn't in the mood for busy work. Instead, she called Marge Pratt and invited her to the movies. Gwenn was as surprised at making the call as Marge was at receiving it. They went to a foreign film—a light, romantic comedy set in the Greek islands. They cried a little and laughed a lot and stopped for an ice-cream soda before parting.

On Sunday, Gwenn slept till noon and was deep in the Sunday *Times* Arts and Leisure section when Al Benjamin called.

"There's good news and there's bad news."

She invited him over.

"Nice building," he commented on entering. "Good location. Well maintained."

"I like it."

He took a turn around the living room, inspecting the Chippendale desk and the Sarouk carpet, two of the items Gwenn had managed to save when bad investments forced her parents to give up the place on Fifth Avenue and auction off most of their possessions. He stopped and looked long at the Kandinsky. He examined her books, accumulated from kindergarten through college, which she'd cared enough about to keep in storage till she found a permanent place with adequate space.

"Nice place. Very nice. I'd like to get a place like this. Rental?"

"No. Condo." Then in answer to his raised eyebrows, she explained. "It was Cordelia's."

"Sure. I knew you were doing good, but not this good."

She grinned. "So? What've you got for me?"

"Not much." He picked out the most comfortable chair and settled himself. "No irregularities. Their profits are down. They should review their operation, bring it up to date. They've been paying a consultant over the years, but I don't see any results. I haven't looked up the reports, but I can do that if you want."

"Is it worthwhile?"

"Couldn't hurt."

A few dollars, more or less, she thought. "Do it. Go ahead."

"Right. There is one thing—a little gossip I picked up. Actually, the rumor's been on the Street for a while. You haven't heard?"

"No."

He was pleased. "It's very hush-hush. There's a likelihood of a takeover."

"Of Triad? By whom?"

"Xenobia."

One of the giants in the oil industry. Her eyebrows went up. "Why should they be interested? What has Triad got that Xenobia could possibly want?"

The accountant put his finger to the side of his nose and winked. Now he was enjoying himself. "Certain holdings in Canada. A secret survey reported there are large oil deposits under one of their fields."

"Oh?"

"Xenobia is making a lucrative offer—an exchange of stock plus a substantial cash settlement. Jessup and Jonathan Trent were in favor; Douglas Trent was against."

"Why? It sounds like a good deal."

"Douglas Trent wanted Triad to explore the field. Based on the findings of the survey, they'd have no trouble raising operating capital. Why bring in an outsider? Why share the profits? Jessup's point, and Jonathan's, was that if they came up empty, they'd lose everything. They'd be wiped out. Why take the risk? With Xenobia in the picture, they couldn't lose."

"Couldn't they outvote Douglas?" Gwenn asked.

"According to the original partnership agreement based on the old man's will, expansion of the partnership required unanimous agreement."

"How about selling part of their shares to Xenobia? It would give Xenobia a foot in the door."

Al Benjamin beamed approvingly. "The buzz on the Street is that's exactly what they intended."

Inevitably the word had got to Douglas, Gwenn thought. He went right up to Toronto to confront his son. And Jonathan backed down. With his son in line, Douglas called for a meeting with Jessup. Jessup checked with Jonathan and found out what had happened. All that stuff about buying land had served as a front.

"Good work, Al."

"I wish I could give you something more definite."

"This will keep me busy for a while."

"I'll get back to you on the consultant."

After Benjamin was gone, Gwenn sat at her desk, legs outstretched, staring out the window at the full moon rising in a black velvet sky. Jonathan Trent had made no bones about needing money. Maybe, as Sheila Trent claimed, his father had promised him a raise, but that would hardly match what he'd get from Xenobia. Jessup's financial situation was unknown to her, but greed was as good a motive as need. So for both Jonathan Trent and Maurice Jessup there would have been only one solution—get rid of Douglas.

Would the son kill his own father? The way Gwenn read him, Jonathan didn't have the stomach for it. Of course, there was no question about who delivered the actual blows. The boys, Paulie and Adam, had done that, but had Jonathan hired them? At long distance? From Toronto? He could hardly have conducted the job interview over the telephone.

And what about Jessup? He must have had some idea of the situation between Douglas and Emma. So he'd looked for someone that could be linked to Emma. He knew about the dance school; Douglas had talked to him about it. Jessup had admitted that much.

Tenuous. Too many assumptions. She didn't like it. So she was back to Adam's suicide note and Paulie's evidence.

Chapter
FOURTEEN

Joyce Hazzlit was trembling. She'd seen him buried. She'd stood at the grave site and watched as the earth was shoveled over the casket spadeful by spadeful. She'd thought she was rid of Douglas Trent at last. She was free. In time, she would forget. She would have her life back.

The phone call was a shock. She panicked and agreed to the demands. What else could she do? Dazed as she was, she had pulled herself together enough to point out to the caller that it would take some time for her to get the money. It hadn't been easy for her to scrape up the initial amount, she told him. She had no more in the bank. But she'd manage, she assured him. She'd get it somehow.

He gave her two days. When he called the next time, she'd better be ready to pay.

Where had he got her telephone number? Joyce Hazzlit wondered. She'd gone to a lot of trouble to avoid just such a situation. She thought she'd made sure he didn't know her name nor where she lived. How had he found out? She'd made the inital contact. She'd called him, told him she had something to discuss that might be to his advantage, and they had agreed to meet. She chose the place. It was near enough to where he lived so he could get there on his bike. She came by car. She got there ahead of him and left after him. She'd made sure to wait till he was gone and out of sight before even walking over to her car. She'd considered the precautions adequate. Evidently, they hadn't been. He was a smart kid. He must have pedaled a ways, then pulled over to wait behind some shrubbery till she drove by. He couldn't have pedaled fast enough to follow her and she would have seen him, but he could have gotten her license number. Once he had that he was well on his way to finding out who she was and where she lived.

What could she do? Put new locks on the door? Move? He'd find her. Even if she had the money, she wouldn't pay him, Joyce Hazzlit thought. He'd only keep coming back for more. She'd lost a lot of years to Douglas Trent, but at last she was rid of him. She hadn't come this far to let a sixteen-year-old addict take over her life.

Her long, slim alabaster hands tipped with beautifully manicured nails trembled as she ran her fingers through her long, platinum hair. She surveyed herself in the antique mirror over the console.

It wasn't too late to start again.

On Monday Gwenn got up early and drove out to Queens to be at the school when the buses arrived and delivered the students. It was the start of the last week of the school year. Summer vacations lay ahead, but nobody was celebrating. There was none of the usual rough and tumble, the good-natured shoving and shouting. They were subdued, almost orderly as they filed inside. One of their classmates had killed himself. Another was awaiting trial as an accessory to murder. Thank God, they weren't inured to the reality of it. They were still children, Gwenn thought. Thank God.

Which among all of these children had been friendly with Adam McClure and Paulie Kellen? Gwenn got out of her car, locked it, and went up the path to the school's main entrance. She showed her ID to the security guard and asked the way to the office of the head of the PT department.

Buzz Grogan's office had been converted from a store-room. It had no windows, so light and air were provided artificially. Team photographs covered the walls. By the style of the uniforms, Gwenn judged some dated back to Grogan's own playing years; others, more recent, were teams he had coached. Framed certificates attested to his various accreditations. An oversized metal desk and filing cabinets took up most of the space. Grogan himself, six foot three and two hundred and twenty pounds, filled what was left. Gwenn sidled in, hoping not to knock over the precariously perched trophies and the stacks of files.

Grogan appraised her with teary pale blue eyes. Realizing he was staring, he broke off. "Sorry, Ms. Ramadge. I never met a lady PI before. In fact, I never met a private investigator before, male or female." Reaching across the desk, he held out a large, meaty hand.

He was older than she had at first thought. His red hair was turning gray. The overhead fluorescent light strip emphasized the deep furrows on his brow and from his nose down to his mouth.

"What can I do for you?"

He gripped her hand so hard she winced. It was no time to dance around the subject, she decided. "You worked with Emma Trent. What do you think of her?"

He pursed his lips, frowned, and then ducked the subject. "To start with, I didn't work with her. Our programs were integrated, but we didn't conduct sessions together. If you follow me."

"I do." He was evading responsibility.

"Personally, I like Emma," he went on to assure Gwenn. "All this talk about her past, her first husband

and how he died, her working in night clubs, mixing with the customers—it's irrelevant, as far as I'm concerned. She came in cold with her proposal. It wasn't original with her, of course. Some of the top colleges in the East, specifically Dartmouth, sponsor a *Dance for Athletes Class.* It included football, hockey, basketball, and soccer players."

"So the concept isn't new?"

"Not at all. However, it hadn't been tried at the high school level. I passed her on to the principal. He was impressed with the idea, her presentation, and her qualifications. We decided to give it a try. It went well. The word got around, and in less than two years team enrollment tripled. She's accomplished a lot. The boys are more limber, their reflexes are sharper. They're more responsive mentally and physically." He paused. "It's very hard for me to believe she would pervert those boys."

"How do you know she did?"

Grogan floundered, but only briefly. "The suicide note."

Of course, Gwenn thought. Naturally. "You know Paulie Kellen pretty well, don't you? And you knew Adam McClure."

"They were both on the basketball team."

"Are you surprised they were capable of committing this terrible, brutal, bloody crime?"

"God, yes." He was sweating profusely.

"Did you know Kellen was doing drugs?"

"I did not." No hesitation or wavering on this. "If I had known, I would have reported it. Nobody does drugs and stays on the team."

"I didn't mean to suggest you would condone it, Mr. Grogan," she assured him and shifted quickly to what she was really after. "Which of the two boys would you say was the leader, Kellen or McClure?"

"Oh, Kellen, of course."

"Are you sure?"

"Ask anybody on the team or in their classes. Adam was transferred from a private school in mid-term. He was timid and he had a hard time fitting in. The kids sensed it. Paulie took on the role of protector. Unless you were prepared to deal with Paulie, you left Adam alone."

"And nobody wanted to take on Paulie," Gwenn concluded.

"Right."

"Doesn't it seem odd, then, that on this occasion, on this very grave enterprise, Adam was the one in charge?"

"Ordinarily, I'd say yes. But if you take into consideration Adam's feelings for Mrs. Trent, that changes everything. A boy with a crush on an older woman, seeing her abused and mistreated . . . anything is possible."

That was the sticking point, Gwenn thought, and somehow she had to get past it.

"So you were aware of Adam's feelings for Mrs. Trent?"

"No. At the beginning I attended classes at the studio. I needed to familiarize myself with her program and her methods. I had to make sure they were appropriate and that we weren't working at cross-purposes. She didn't pay any more attention to Adam than to any of the others. The team came in a group and left in a group. It's possible they saw each other afterwards. I don't know."

"Do you think any of the boys knew how Adam felt?"

"I don't think so. Except for Paulie, probably. Adam told Paulie everything."

The station was rarely frequented. Most of the trains heading for Brooklyn and Manhattan passed straight through without stopping. The station house, with its ticket office, waiting room, and toilets, had long since been shut down to discourage vagrants and vandals. All that was left was a shed on each side of the tracks in which passengers might be sheltered from the wind and rain. There were a couple of slatted benches in the open. Most of the platform lights were either burned out or broken. It was a desolate place. On this night in late June, it seemed more so because of the fog that hung wet and heavy over it.

The station was surrounded by apartment buildings, well maintained, middle class, occupied by responsible citizens. Occasionally, a gust of wind parted the curtain of fog and a solitary figure sitting slumped on one of the benches was revealed. Waiting for a train? No trains stopped at that hour. If the man didn't know that, he'd find out. Nobody was going to take it on himself to inform him. Not far from here, Kitty Genovese had screamed for help and not one of those responsible, middle-class citizens in the staid buildings had answered the call till it was too late. Their collective guilt was a palpable essence along with the fog.

It was shortly after midnight that Norman Strummer, covered with the accumulated sweat and dirt of the days since he'd used a public washroom, left hand trembling, dragging the black plastic trash bag that held his wordly possessions, approached the figure on the bench.

"Hey, you!" he snarled. "This is where I sleep. This is my space."

No answer.

"You deaf? Move it. I said, move it."

Still no response. Exasperated, Strummer leaned over and shoved the usurper toward the end of the bench.

"Git!"

One more shove, and the figure toppled over to the pavement. Strummer opened the plastic sack and took out a threadbare blanket he'd retrieved from a trash bin only a few days ago. Stretching on the bench he'd just cleared, he draped it over himself. The bag, with the rest of its contents, he placed under his head to serve as a pillow and also to ensure no one could steal his belongings. Settled, he closed his eyes and quickly fell asleep. The man he'd displaced lay on the pavement where he'd fallen.

It was five A.M. when the sanitation crew spotted the two. They didn't bother to go down and take a closer look. It was their job to pick up trash, and there was no trash down there. It wasn't their job to chase vagrants. They reported to railroad security that there were a couple of homeless persons sleeping on company property. That ended their responsibility. In due course somebody would be over to remove them. That was the new policy. The passengers were losing compassion. Impatience, even fear, was taking its place. However, Security was instructed that in clearing out the unwanted, they should not leave the company open to charges of violating their civil rights. Therefore, Security in turn notified Human Resources. HR, on this morning as on all others, was fully occupied with the routine of bussing clients from the shelters where they had spent the night to the various institutions that would serve them breakfast. Meanwhile, during the entire rush hour, the paying customers of the railroad looked askance at the two huddled forms and took care to give them a wide berth.

It was late morning when the HR team arrived. It was then discovered that one of the two, the one on the pavement—young, male, Caucasian—was not homeless. He was dead.

Response time was faster for death than for life. The first RMP car arrived within five minutes of the call from the HR team. As soon as the victim's ID was established, not a difficult task since he carried his student pass, the usual police notifications were made, starting with Homicide. The connection to the Trent case discovered, Sergeant Dixon went to the scene. He was dismayed and saddened. He was also perplexed.

Paul Kellen, Jr., lay on the pavement, huddled in on himself, knees drawn up and hands folded across his chest. He had been shot in the back at close range with a small caliber gun, very likely a .22. He had been shot several times, the bullets pumped into him. They had all been in the same area, so the wound was large and irregular in shape. Dixon bent over and positioned himself so he could look into the dead boy's face. His eyes were wide open. In surprise?

According to the ME's preliminary estimate, death had occurred about twelve hours previous, making it about eleven or twelve the night before.

As a witness, Norman Strummer was nearly useless. Dixon tried anyway; he was all they had. "What time did you get here?" he asked the homeless man.

"I don't know." Strummer shook all over. "I don't own a watch, man. I had one once. Yeah, I did. But they stole it off me. At the shelter."

Paulie Kellen had been shot in the middle of the back, but the impact wouldn't have been powerful enough to knock him off the bench. "Was he on the ground like that when you got here?"

"Huh?" The homeless man looked straight into Dixon's face and for seconds the trembling stopped and he became absolutely still.

He had put it badly, Dixon thought. "Was he already here when you arrived?"

"I guess so." Gradually, the twitching began again.

"What was he doing?"

"Nothing. Sitting."

"Where?"

"On the bench. On my bench. I didn't do nothing. He was on my bench. I told him so. I told him to get off." Norman Strummer was shaking violently. "I'm not a bad person, but it was my bench. That's where I sleep. I pushed him over to make room, that's all." Bending his right arm, he managed to demonstrate. "It's not my fault he's dead. I didn't do nothing to hurt him," he pleaded.

"Of course not," Dixon soothed. So Paulie Kellen was already dead when the homeless man got there. He had been sitting on the bench doing nothing, as Strummer indicated. Waiting. The person he'd been waiting for had crept up on him and shot him in the back.

"And you have no idea what time it was when you got here?"

"Sure I do." Strummer smiled smugly. "It was time to sleep. Time to sleep."

"It's easy to pin it on Emma Trent," Gwenn declared hotly. "It saves all kinds of trouble."

She sat with Ray in a booth at the rear of a small neighborhood bar and grill not far from the station house. Lew had called her a couple of hours earlier to tell her about Paulie Kellen's death. He also told her that his father had suffered yet another heart attack and he was rushing to Miami to be with him. Upset as he was, Gwenn hadn't felt right about quizzing him for details of the crime and how it would affect Emma. She'd called Dixon, and he had readily agreed to meet her.

When she arrived, he was there and waiting. It was still early, so the place was just about empty. The lights were low; soft music was piped in as background. He offered her a drink.

"Coffee, thanks."

"Sure you don't want something stronger?"

"No, thanks." She was impatient to get on with it. "I don't drink in the afternoon."

"Neither do I," he retorted. "I thought a drink might relax you."

I wasn't tense till I came in here, Gwenn thought, but didn't say it. It seemed that with every word the atmosphere became more strained. Somehow, she couldn't hit the right note with this man. "Coffee will be fine."

"Whatever you say. Two coffees." He dismissed the waitress.

"Should we stick to the case without getting personal?" she asked.

"We can try. Has it ever occurred to you, Miss Ramadge, that you're prejudiced?"

"Prejudiced? Me? If believing in someone's innocence is being prejudiced, then okay, I am. I think that's a lot better than taking a person's guilt for granted."

"If I were doing that, your client would be back in jail by now. She's not."

"That's very magnanimous of you."

"Don't thank me, thank the DA. It's his decision. He hasn't made up his mind on which charge to try her."

"Depending on the evidence you turn," she insisted.

"He has his own investigators."

"Who are just as willing as you to take the easy way."

Dixon's color deepened. "I don't think you really mean that."

"No, I don't. I'm sorry. I apologize."

Their eyes met. She saw that she had really hurt him. He saw she was genuinely sorry. They both smiled tentatively.

"You know what?" Dixon asked. "If I'm ever in trouble, I want you on my team."

"Thank you."

The moment passed.

"The thing is, Emma had no motive for killing Paulie Kellen," Gwenn said.

"What? You've got to be kidding."

"No, listen. Just listen," Gwenn urged. "She's already charged with solicitation of murder. What more did she have to fear from Paulie?"

"The accusation came from the other kid, from Adam. He's dead. He can't stand up in court and point a finger at her."

"He's pointing a finger at her from the grave," Gwenn retorted. "That's worse."

The waitress brought their coffees. Dixon waited till she was gone.

"Actually, the note was ambiguous. It's subject to interpretation."

Gwenn caught her breath. He recognized it and was willing to admit it!

"Paulie could have corroborated the note."

"But he didn't," she pointed out. "He didn't say one word to involve Emma Trent."

"Of course not. He was saving that. If things looked really bad for him, that was his ace in the hole."

"I suppose . . . All right, but why should she feel threatened all of a sudden?"

"Come on, you know the answer as well as I do. Paulie tried to blackmail her, of course. The kid was an addict. Addicts always need money. They never have enough."

Gwenn bowed her head; she'd run out of objections. Then, suddenly, she raised it again. "It's a moot point anyway. We know she didn't do it. She has an alibi."

"She has?"

"Of course. He was shot last night, right? Well, Thursday through Sunday she was under police protection. Lew spent the night downstairs in her living room and squad cars were parked front and rear till Monday morning," she announced with satisfaction. "They can vouch for her."

"I'm afraid not. She wasn't seen going out, but she was seen coming back in. The men stationed at the rear

reported seeing her coming through a neighbor's backyard to her own backyard and into the house by way of
the kitchen at a quarter past midnight last night. Kellen
was shot between eleven P.M. and one A.M. I'm sorry,"
he added, and he truly was.

The news stunned Gwenn. "Did Lew know about
this?"

"Yes. I'm sure he meant to tell you, but he was very
upset about his father. All he was thinking about was
getting to his bedside."

"Of course," she said and struggled to recover. "How
come nobody saw Mrs. Trent go out?"

"There was an accident. A kid got knocked off his
bike by a passing motorist. The officers from the back
went around to give assistance. An ambulance came;
more RMPs; the whole street turned out. You know
how it is. During the commotion, she was able to slip
away."

Gwenn had herself in hand again. "She couldn't have
known it was going to happen. I hope you're not suggesting she set it up?"

"I'm suggesting she took advantage of the opportunity.
Once out, she contacted Paulie Kellen and they arranged
to meet."

"And what does she say? I assume you've talked to
her."

"She admits to taking advantage of the distraction to
get out of the house. She felt cooped up, she said. She
had cabin fever. She needed to walk around on her own,
to breathe without being watched."

"That's not hard to understand."

"The accident occurred at ten-eighteen P.M. She had
plenty of time to call Kellen, get over to the station,
do what had to be done and get back," Dixon pointed
out. "She claims she just took a walk along Austin
Street. Unfortunately, she didn't talk to anybody; she

didn't stop anywhere for a bite or a drink. Nobody saw her. In my opinion, she's the prime suspect in both murders."

"But...?" Gwenn challenged.

"We haven't turned the murder weapon."

Chapter————
————FIFTEEN

At least there was no hard evidence against Emma, Gwenn thought, but once again she was faced with trying to prove a negative.

The bar was starting to fill up. The conversation level rose, drowning out the Muzak. She had to lean across the table to make herself heard.

"I'm sorry I snapped, Ray. You've got your job to do. I understand." She held out her hand.

"And you've got yours." He took it. "How about something to eat? I've got to get back to the squad, but we could have something here. The food's pretty good."

"No, thanks...." She stopped. She must not be so abrupt. The fact was, she didn't know why she was so resistant. It couldn't be because of his name; she had long since got over that coincidence. In fact, he was nothing like that other Ray. The other Ray flaunted his looks. Ray Dixon was just as good looking, but he almost apologized for it. Ray, the photographer, was unscrupulous in his drive for success. Ray Dixon was determined, but was careful about using people. So, granting all that, why was she always so tense with him? Why did she maintain a distance?

"That would be nice, but I have to get home. I'm expecting... Lew said he'd call as soon as he got in."

"Sure."

"Well, thank you for talking to me. I appreciate it."
Gwenn slid around the table and stood up.

Dixon stayed where he was. "How long have you
known Lew?"

The question was unexpected. "A little over a year.
We worked on a case. After it was over, we didn't see
each other for a while." Now why had she told him that?

Dixon got up, too. They walked to the front and Dixon
paid their bill. Then he saw her to her car.

"Thanks again," she said.

"Any time. If there's anything else you need, give me
a call ... while Lew's away."

She flushed. What was that supposed to mean?

Firmly, Gwenn put Ray Dixon out of her mind. She was
expecting a call from Lew, but not till later. She went
home anyway; she had nowhere else to go. As she was
looking over the contents of her refrigerator, deciding
what to fix for dinner, the phone rang. It was Lew. Mental telepathy?

His father was better, Lew said. The doctors were
pleased. But they were going to keep him under obser-
vation for at least a week and Lew was going to stay with
him, just to be sure.

"Of course. You should do that, absolutely," she
agreed.

"How was your meeting with Ray?"

The question took her by surprise. "How did you know
we had a meeting?"

"He called me."

"He did? Where? At the hospital?"

"That's right."

"When?"

"Half an hour ago."

"Did he tell you I was expecting to hear from you?"

"Yes."

"And what did you say?"

"I said I intended to call. In fact, I was just on the verge. What's going on?"

"Nothing. What does Ray say about the case?"

"Says things don't look so good for Mrs. Trent, but you're determined to stand by her. I told him I wasn't surprised."

"Thanks, Lew."

"Loyalty can go too far, you know."

"I know."

He grunted. "I hope so. If you get any bright ideas, talk to Ray first, okay? No one-on-one confrontations. Promise?"

Who was there to confront? Gwenn asked herself as she sat at the kitchen table, eating the chef's salad she'd put together from the various leftovers. The investigation of Triad had revealed all was not what it seemed at Triad. There was dissension between the partners. Resentment on the part of Trent's son. In her own mind, Gwenn had eliminated Jonathan and she didn't have enough evidence to warrant an accusation against Jessup. Douglas Trent's personal life was a sham. According to friends and associates, his marriage was happy, but, in reality, it was a nightmare. That was the second marriage, Gwenn reminded herself. How about the first? It was supposed to have been idyllic.

But had it been?

Gwenn burned with excitement. All of a sudden, the first marriage loomed all-important. Who was the most likely to know? Who would be willing to tell her?

Maurice Jessup had already taken the position that the first marriage had been made in heaven. No use interrogating him again; he was not likely to waver unless she had something new to use as leverage. Same applied to Rachel Montrone, Trent's secretary. She'd been with Trent for a lot of years and was the most likely to know whatever there was to know. But she was loyal to the point of stubbornness. Gwenn smiled; that's what Lew had accused her of. So, if no one was going to tell her, she would have to find out for herself. She rinsed the dishes and put them in the dishwasher. Then she went in to change.

She put on the standard outfit for this kind of job—navy slacks, navy pullover, black Reeboks. She checked the contents of her worn black leather pouch: small flashlight—working; two cameras—batteries charged; fresh pair of cotton gloves. How about the piece? Would she need it? She decided she wouldn't. She had no intention of being discovered. But if luck should turn against her, there was no reason for a shoot-out. Cordelia had always preached against illegal entry for a variety of reasons. Gwenn agreed and added her own postscript: if caught, surrender gracefully.

She left her apartment and walked over to Fifth Avenue, caught a downtown bus to Forty-fourth, then walked over toward Sixth.

Triad Paper occupied the entire third floor of a small office building about a quarter of the way over from the corner. The lights were out. In fact, except for a dim glow in the lobby, the entire building was dark. A table was set facing the plate-glass door. It held an open ledger, the sign-in book. Seated at the table was a stout, balding man in slacks and a plaid shirt: the night watchman. Sometime he would make rounds, but when?

Gwenn crossed the street to a small coffee shop and took a stool at the counter from where she could observe. Sipping her coffee, she watched and waited. After about twenty minutes a delivery boy carrying a flat pizza box approached the door and rang the bell. The watchman got up and unlocked it. He accepted the delivery, paid for it, and locked up again. Then he sat down to his meal.

It would be a while till he moved, if he moved at all, Gwenn decided. She paid and left.

There had to be a service entrance, she thought as she strolled along the rest of the block, but she couldn't find what she was looking for. She turned the corner and started back on the other side and discovered a narrow alley and at the back a pair of metal doors. On one, the lock appeared to have already been tampered with, apparently unsuccessfully. She took out her set of picks to try her luck. The lock responded quickly and easily. The door swung open. With a quick look over her shoulder, Gwenn Ramadge stepped inside.

The service elevator was at ground level and invitingly open. If she used it, in the silence of the building, the watchman would surely hear it. So, it was the stairs. Making sure to set the lock so that she wouldn't be trapped inside the stairwell, Gwenn climbed. Three flights shouldn't have been tiring, but by the time she reached the Triad offices, she was breathing heavily. Nerves. The main entrance to the suite was also locked, of course. With the small penlight in her mouth so both hands were free, she probed. It wasn't as easy as it had been downstairs. She felt queasy. Just because security was slack down below was no reason to assume it was so up here. It might for that reason be very sophisticated. Triad might be protected by a photocell system or a silent alarm. She might already have activated it. She stood still and held her breath. At any moment police and private security guards could be swarming all over the place. Her heart thundered. She wasn't cut out for this kind of thing.

But nothing happened.

Of course not, she told herself. They didn't keep anything of value here. Therefore, they didn't require elaborate, expensive protection. Even if such a system were in place, she still had plenty of time to get away before anybody responded. At that very moment she felt the tumblers in the lock click, and the knob turned in her hand.

She found her way to Douglas Trent's office; it wasn't locked. She closed the window blinds, turned on the desk lamp, and settled herself in his chair. She was looking for personal data: an address book, an appointment diary. Everybody relied on some sort of memo. There had been nothing like that in his home, so it had to be here— unless it had already been removed. *Don't think about that. Think positive.*

Twenty-five minutes later, having found what she wanted, Gwenn was ready to leave. As she emerged from the alley, she realized she was sweating. The evidence she had placed in her black leather pouch opened an entire new avenue for investigation. It was still early, but even if it had been much later, she had no intention of putting the interview off till morning. She hailed a cab and gave the driver Rachel Montrone's address.

The secretary lived in the Lincoln Center area in a new, expensive high rise. How could she afford it? Gwenn wondered as a stiffly elegant doorman approached her, at the same time barring her way. She had no choice but to give her name and let him announce her.

"Miss Montrone has retired," he informed her.

"Tell her it's very important."

The doorman raised both eyebrows, but he picked up the house phone a second time.

"She'll see you in the morning."

"That'll be too late, tell her. Here, let me speak to

her." Gwenn held out her hand for the receiver, but he didn't relinquish it. "Tell her if she doesn't speak to me now she'll have to speak to the police."

He gaped. The authority bestowed on him by the uniform was vitiated. He relayed the message, word for word, humbly, almost urging compliance.

"Please go up, miss," he told Gwenn. "Apartment 14E." He waved her toward the elevator, where the operator sprang to his feet to serve her.

Rachel Montrone opened the door promptly. She must have been standing right there waiting, Gwenn thought. She was wearing a ruby velvet robe trimmed with lace at the collar and wrists. She had washed off her makeup and her hair fell loosely around her pale face. Despite the gray in her hair and the dark circles under her eyes, the secretary looked younger than she had in the office interview.

"What's happened?"

Gwenn walked past her into the living room and looked around. It was small but luxuriously decorated in shades of mauve and pale green, bathed in soft, indirect lighting. Very feminine. Whereas her office had been rigidly impersonal, even austere, here Rachel Montrone was surrounded by memorabilia; photographs in fancy frames abounded. A collection of ivory and ebony elephants carved in various styles and sizes marched across the shelves of a display cabinet.

"What's happened?" Rachel Montrone asked again.

Gwenn took a small leather-bound notebook from her pouch and held it out.

Montrone didn't touch it. "Where did you get that?"

"You recognize it?"

"It's Mr. Trent's personal appointment book. What about it?"

"Certain entries need to be explained."

"All right." The secretary took a deep breath. "I'll do my best, but why all the urgency? Barging in like this?

Threatening to call the police? I don't know what my doorman thinks. Whatever it is, he'll spread it through the whole building."

"You've been holding out on me, Miss Montrone," Gwenn chided. "You haven't told the truth."

"I've answered all your questions."

"That's not quite the same. Evasion can be tantamount to lying. For example, you never told me about this book."

A nerve twitched below her left eye, but the secretary was far from surrendering. "The book is an abbreviated version of Mr. Trent's appointment schedule that he carried with him. I answered what you asked, but I forgot about the book."

"I don't think so, Miss Montrone. There are entries in this book that are not in the office appointment calendar. You kept a record of Mr. Trent's business dates, of course, that was your job." She held up the notebook. "But these other entries . . . I have to assume they're no secret to you since you had to reconcile the two."

Rachel Montrone sank slowly into the nearest chair and put a hand up over her eyes.

Gwenn sat opposite. "The last entry is for May 31. It says simply: Kennedy, AA 5:45 P.M. I take that to refer to his American Airlines flight to Toronto."

"That's right."

"He didn't take the book with him."

"He didn't need it. The agenda for his visit was handled up there."

Gwenn turned some pages. "The initials JH appear on an average of once a week. Who is JH?"

"A friend."

"I see that when he met JH for lunch there was seldom any other appointment scheduled for later that afternoon."

"I hadn't noticed."

"You can stop protecting him, Rachel."

"I'm not."

"Loyalty to your boss when he was alive is one thing. I'm not sure he deserved it, but that's not for me to say. He's dead now. Everyone's suffered enough. Including you, I think. Who is JH?"

"Joyce Hazzlit," Rachel Montrone murmured. "She was...his mistress."

An old-fashioned word, Gwenn thought. A term which implied a stable, if not permanent, relationship. She might have said: girlfriend, lover, roommate. *Mistress* suggested the man was supporting the woman and doing so in a certain degree of luxury. Gwenn continued to leaf through the notebook. "It appears he's been seeing her at least since the beginning of the year. The book doesn't go any farther back."

"They'd been together for many years, going back to before Lucille Trent's death."

Gwenn remained impassive. "Before her illness?"

"Yes."

Rachel Montrone's eyes, however, gleamed. As she spoke, her careful reserve, the curtain behind which she'd been hiding, was torn. "Lucille was not the loving helpmate she was made out to be. I'm not talking about when she was sick and I'm not minimizing her suffering. I'm talking about the person she was. She inherited the business from her father. It was hers and she never let Douglas forget that. She made him toe the line at home and at work. She could override any business decision he might make. She didn't do it often, but enough so that the occasion was significant and etched in everyone's memory. Usually she chose a matter over which the partners were divided and sided with Mr. Jessup. It was a calculated move, designed to humiliate."

Still defending him, Gwenn thought. "You cared for him, didn't you?" she asked gently.

Once again that telltale twitch. She had kept it covered so long, had denied it so many times, especially to herself, that denial was automatic. "There was nothing between us."

"But you loved him and he knew it," Gwenn insisted. *He knew it and enjoyed it,* she thought.

"No."

"His response was to flaunt the other woman."

"He never did any such thing."

"Then how did you know about Joyce Hazzlit?"

"I had to know where to reach him, didn't I? In case of emergency?"

"Particularly when his wife became critical."

The secretary looked away.

"So you had Miss Hazzlit's address and telephone number. Did Mr. Trent ever order you to send flowers?" Each question added to Rachel Montrone's pain. It saddened Gwenn, but she had to continue. "How about her bills? Charge accounts? Did he pay her rent?" She'd been letting instinct guide her from one question to the next, and suddenly she'd struck pay dirt. "You paid her bills out of company funds!"

"Lucille kept him on a tight string. He had to account for every check he drew."

Still on his side. "How? How was it done?" she asked, though she thought she knew.

There was a long pause. "She was on the books as a consultant," Montrone whispered. "Hazzlit Associates."

Gwenn heard and was sorry for her. It was the old, sad story—a decent woman corrupted by loving the wrong man.

"What could I do?" Montrone pleaded. "I had to go along with it. I didn't want to lose my job. I was too old to start over in the steno pool. Who would want me?"

She might be too old now, but she hadn't been then, Gwenn thought, and looked from the secretary in her robe of velvet and lace to her luxurious apartment crammed with expensive possessions. "So while you were at it, you took something for yourself."

"Why not? He owed me."

So much for romance. "Neither of you was in a position to inform on the other."

Montrone shrugged.

"Were you surprised that after Lucille's death, Douglas Trent didn't marry his girlfriend?"

"I was at first. Then I realized he didn't really love her. She'd been a . . . convenience."

Gwenn nearly smiled. An old-fashioned lady indeed. An innocent, really. Then it struck her. "You thought he might turn to you."

"No." She answered too quickly.

"You did. At least for a moment, for one fleeting moment, you allowed yourself to think so. Be honest, Rachel, didn't you just for a little while permit yourself to dream?"

"No. I was too old. Not glamorous enough. I'd stopped dreaming a long time ago."

Her resignation was totally believable; nevertheless, Gwenn had to follow the lead. "What did you think when you found out Douglas had resumed the affair with his old flame?" She held the appointment diary in her hand to remind Rachel Montrone denial would be a waste of time.

"I didn't know what to think."

Gwenn expected more rationalizing, but the secretary was silent.

"How about the new wife? Do you think Emma Trent knew about the affair?"

"I couldn't say. But if she did, it would be a strong motive for having him killed."

Gwenn nodded. Every lead came back to Emma.

Chapter

SIXTEEN

It must have rained in the night, Gwenn thought, looking out her window. The morning was fresh, scrubbed clean; the pollution, wrung out of the air. Strong winds cleared the last of the grimy haze. Everything had a hard, sharp edge. Gwenn Ramadge herself felt renewed and eager. Joyce Hazzlit was a new factor in the case, and Gwenn couldn't wait to find out more about her. Trent's mistress lived on East End Avenue near Gracie Mansion, and the first order of business was to go up there and look around, talk to her neighbors, find out as much as possible about her lifestyle before approaching her directly. Her outfit of the day consisted of beige slacks and a navy linen blazer—suitable for any situation. Before leaving the house, Gwenn remembered to call Marge and tell her what she was up to.

It wasn't far and she decided to walk. She set out briskly and by the time she reached Carl Schurz Park, she felt pleasantly exhilarated. She sat on a bench near the entrance and leaned back to absorb the atmosphere. The pace was slow. People strolled, walked their dogs; mothers pushed baby carriages. The hot-dog vendor on the corner was doing good business, as was the balloon man. The mayor's mansion, situated on its well-tended grounds overlooking the estuary waters, set the tone for the entire neighborhood. The new branch of Beth Israel, Beth Israel Hospital North, added a sense of commitment. The residential buildings themselves presented a variety of styles and economic condition. Joyce Hazzlit lived in a remodeled, very modern edifice on the corner. There was no doorman. Gwenn watched as a couple of deliveries were made, residents admitting themselves with a passkey. Then she crossed over to take a closer look. There was, as she'd guessed, a closed circuit television. She scanned the tenant roster in the vestibule. J. Hazzlit was in apartment 4A.

She could ring, be admitted on some pretext or other, and go upstairs. Then what? The woman, if she was at home, didn't have to talk to Gwenn. Didn't have to answer her questions or tell her one damn thing. In fact, Gwenn often marveled at how readily people did talk to her, did unburden themselves, when, in fact, she had no official standing. Why should Ms. Hazzlit, who had kept her relationship with Douglas Trent secret for years, who had managed to remain anonymous throughout a murder investigation, now open up and reveal herself to a stranger on her doorstep? Why shouldn't she just slam the door in her face? If the positions were reversed, that's what Gwenn would do. What she had to do was make Joyce Hazzlit *want* to see her, *want* to talk to her. Better yet would be if she could make Hazzlit seek her out. Three weeks had passed since the murder of Douglas Trent, and the police hadn't come anywhere near Joyce Hazzlit. She must be feeling secure. She needed shaking up.

Without further analysis or a detailed plan, Gwenn acted, confident her intuition would guide her when the moment came. She left the building and walked around the corner to a telephone booth she'd noticed on the way over. She dropped a quarter in the slot and dialed. The phone rang three times and then was picked up.

"Hello?"

The voice was light, airy. How much could be gleaned from one word? Gwenn didn't speak.

"Hello?" Joyce Hazzlit repeated with a touch of impatience, and something more. "Hello?"

Still Gwenn Ramadge remained silent.

"Who is this? What do you want?"

Definitely, agitation replaced annoyance, Gwenn thought; nevertheless, it was time to hang up. She waited five minutes by her watch, then dialed again. This time the receiver was picked up in the middle of the second ring.

"Hello?" The voice was stronger. It hovered at the edge of irritation. "Yes? Who is this?"

As before, Gwenn said nothing.

"What do you want?"

Gwenn hung up and left the booth. She didn't know how long it would take to soften up Joyce Hazzlit. If she was right and the woman had been subjected to this kind of harassment before, it wouldn't be long. It was important not to push too hard or act too soon. Meanwhile, she needed to know as much as possible about the subject: what she looked like, where she worked, what she did with her spare time, who her friends were—in other words, what her life was apart from her relationship with Douglas Trent. Surely, she had another life. What was she doing on a fine day like this, for example? Would she be out strolling through the park enjoying the breeze off the water? This was really a nice place to live, Gwenn thought. And you couldn't pick a better day for hunting for an apartment. Smiling to herself, she went back to Joyce Hazzlit's building and rang the bell for the super.

The intercom crackled. "Yes?"

She spoke into the mouthpiece. "I'm here about the apartment."

"What apartment? We have no vacancies."

"Sure you do. One of your tenants tipped me off."

"Well, whoever told you made a mistake. We have no vacancies."

"Oh?" Gwenn sounded dejected. "Wait, wait. Hold it. I see the problem. This would be a sublet. That's why you don't know about it."

"Nobody sublets without getting permission from the building management firm and they tell me."

"Gee, I'm sorry. I don't want to get anybody into trouble . . ."

The super had hung up.

Gwenn waited and was gratified to hear the slamming of a door at the rear of the first floor hall. Heavy footsteps approached. The lobby door opened and a squat, sturdy man in his early sixties stood on the threshold. His hair was dark and thick, his skin pockmarked. Scraggy eyebrows overhung dark eyes that narrowed as he squinted into the sun to get a good look at her. He wore crisp, clean, gray fatigues with the name Toni stitched in red on his shirt pocket.

"Who's supposed to be subletting?"

"I don't know. Look, I'm sorry. I got this second-hand." Gwenn was very apologetic. "I work in City Hall and I heard through the grapevine that somebody in this building was looking to sublet. I don't know the name of the tenant or I would have gone direct. I don't even know which apartment, though I think it's on the fourth floor." She paused. "You know how tough it is to find a nice place in this city, particularly a rental. The real estate market is supposed to be soft, but I'm here to tell you it's not soft enough. I came in the hope of beating the crowd." She hesitated. "I expect to pay a finder's fee, naturally."

He cleared his throat. "There are two apartments on every floor. On the fourth, we've got Mr. Elton Krauss. He's eighty-three and there's only one way he's ever going to leave this building. Then there's Miss Hazzlit. She travels. Could be her."

"Is she away for long periods of time?"

"I've never known her to be gone more than a couple of weeks to a month at a time. But you never know. She's a model. Does hands. Can you imagine earning a living by having your hands photographed?"

"What agency does she work for?"

She could see the question made him suspicious. "I have contacts with some of the agencies because of my PR work," she explained. "I thought I could get one of them to introduce me to Miss . . . Hazzlit."

"If you want my advice . . ."

"Oh, I do."

"Go to the building management company, Shirer and Smith, and fill out a rental application. Tell them you're willing to take a sublet. You'll be the first on the list." His eyes fixed on hers. "I promise."

"Well, thank you. I'll do that. Could I ask you about the apartment? Is it large?"

"One bedroom."

"Does it face front?"

He nodded. "Overlooking the park and the water."

"That's really nice. If there's one thing I hate it's facing a court; you can't even tell what the weather's like."

They shook hands and Gwenn left.

She had no doubt the super would ask Joyce Hazzlit about her intention to sublet. Usually, Gwenn tried to keep the subject from knowing he was being investigated, but this time she wanted Joyce Hazzlit to find out, and if the super didn't tell her, she was going to make sure somebody else did. From the sidewalk, she looked up to the fourth floor windows she now knew to be Hazzlit's. She was itching to face this woman. She had a plan, a good one, but if she moved too soon, she'd blow it. Resolutely, she started back. Meandering through the side streets in a zigzag pattern, she enjoyed the variety of cultures represented by a Hungarian church, several Viennese pastry shops, and a German Bauhaus. A multitude of Asian establishments—restaurants and fruit and vegetable markets—flourished on First and Second avenues. They enriched the country that had taken them in, she thought as she reached her own block. In spite of crime and the breakdown of services, in spite of racism and corruption, New York was still a great city and she had no desire to be anywhere else. With all of that, she liked her job. She was lucky, she kept assuring her parents, who never stopped trying to get her to move to Cuernavaca with them.

True, she was lonely sometimes, like now for instance. She missed having someone to talk to and confide in. She missed Lew. She could call him in Miami, but she didn't want to bother him when he was so worried about his father. When she got home and saw the red light on her answering machine blinking, her heart jumped. Before she could press the Message button, the phone rang.

"Gwenn, it's me. How are you?"

"Fine. How are you? How's your father?"

"Better. Much better. They're talking about sending him home in a few days."

"That's wonderful!"

"Yes, it is."

But he didn't sound happy, she thought.

"The thing is I want to stay here and see him settled. He's going to need home care."

"Of course. They have social services down there, don't they?"

"Sure. Arrangements are being made for a therapist and a housekeeper. But I want to make sure everything's in place."

"Naturally."

"So it'll probably be another week before I get back."

"As long as it takes. Your father has top priority."

"Right." He took a deep, deep breath. "So what's new up there? Anything on the case?"

"It turns out Trent had a girlfriend on the side. The affair goes back to his first marriage, was suspended when he married Emma—temporarily. It resumed six months later."

"Busy man. Should take some of the pressure off Emma. Unless the girlfriend has a real strong alibi."

He referred to the night of Paulie Kellen's death, Gwenn realized. She hadn't considered the matter of Joyce Hazzlit's alibi. "I don't know," she admitted. "I haven't talked to her yet. I've been too busy on background."

"That's good. Very good. Let Ray handle the interrogation."

"You don't think I'm up to it?"

"I didn't say that. I didn't mean that. Don't be so sensitive."

An experienced investigator would have probed for the alibi before wasting time on matters that might prove irrelevant. She knew that much, Gwenn thought. She must have subconsciously already decided Joyce Hazzlit was guilty. That was wrong and made her touchy.

"Gwenn? I'm sorry. I just don't want you to do anything foolish, that's all."

"Oh? Thank you for your confidence."

"I didn't mean that, either. I mean, don't go rushing in half cocked."

"Gee, that's much better."

There was a pause. Then they both started to laugh.

"You just take care of yourself," Lew urged her in parting. "I worry about you."

"The affair lasted over a period of twelve years," Gwenn explained to Marge Pratt. "Joyce Hazzlit isn't young anymore. She's no cover girl, if she ever was. According to the building super, she does hands."

Gwenn had spent the night compiling a list of model and film actors agencies with offices in New York. She came in early the next morning, surprising Marge Pratt, and divided the list between them.

"Hands," Marge Pratt repeated, eyes bright. Some considered telephone canvassing a bore, but to her it was exciting. Every new number dialed and every new person that answered might be the lead that would break the case.

"It's the one specific we have. If they don't have her listed under 'hands,' ask them to go through their *Character* file. She might fit the housewife type, or the nosy neighbor, or who knows what else?"

"Why are we asking?"

Good question, Gwenn thought. She was pleased. Marge was not only eager to take on the job, but she seemed to have a natural aptitude for it. She'd have to use her more often. "Say we want to hire her. We're a small agency just starting and we can't afford high priced models. We hear Hazzlit is good and she works near scale."

"Yes, ma'am." Marge grinned and punched up the number for the first query.

By lunch they'd located the agency. Joyce Hazzlit was booked through Bi-Coastal Representation.

"Do we want to interview her?" Marge had Bi-Coastal on hold and now stood in the doorway of Gwenn's office. "Because she's not available today or tomorrow. She's working as a dress extra on location at Tavern on the Green."

"Tell them the photos will be sufficient."

"Of the hands?"

Gwenn's eyes met the younger woman's. "Yes, of course, the hands. But we might as well have some head shots and a composite." It was what she was really after. "Tell them to messenger it over."

Marge went out and returned quickly. "They want to know if we'd be interested in any other models. Hazzlit's starting to show her age."

"Tell them it's her hands we're principally interested in."

"It's her hands they're talking about."

Within an hour they knew what Joyce Hazzlit looked like. She was a pale Nordic type. Her silver-blond hair was long and straight and silky, swept back from a high brow. Her skin was fair, translucent. Her face was sculptured, accentuated by high cheek bones with hollow shadows beneath. Her eyes, deep set, were dark pools. In the head shot, she looked about thirty. Since her affair with Trent covered a twelve-year span, that would make her eighteen at the start. Young to be mired in that kind of a relationship. However, her youth might be an explanation in part, at least, of why, when it had started to sour and Douglas began abusing her, she submitted and stayed with him. She was probably older. It didn't matter; the main thing was that she would be easy to identify and to keep in view.

Gwenn had no idea how long the surveillance would last. She had Marge send out for coffee and sandwiches to take with her. Marge was to stay in the office till five as usual. Then she was to go home and stay near the telephone.

"I hope I'm not spoiling your evening."

"I haven't got anything on," Marge assured her. If she had, she would have canceled it.

Security was always tight when a movie was being shot on location. It had to be or no work would get done. Anticipating that, Gwenn had selected from the various cards she carried the one identifying her as a representative of the Mayor's Office for Film and Television Production. She drove up and showed it to the guard at the barricade and was not only passed through but directed to a reserved parking place.

By his harried manner and his clipboard, Gwenn recognized an assistant director.

"Can you tell me who's in charge of the extras?"

"Fred March." He gestured vaguely toward one of the row of trailers that were parked on the road just beyond the famous restaurant.

Gwenn walked over. "I'm looking for Joyce Hazzlit."

March thumbed through the sheets on his board. "Hazzlit, right; she's here. But you can't talk to her. She's on the set."

Gwenn held up the card that had got her in. "This will only take a minute, I promise. Come on, be a sport, Mr. March, I've got to talk to her."

"We're ready to roll, for God's sake."

"I'll wait."

He glared at her, then shrugged. "Wait if you want. It could be hours." He avoided further arguments by simply walking away.

This was not the first time Gwenn had been on a movie set and she knew the delays were unpredictable. Ready to roll could mean anywhere between one minute to one hour and even more. According to the attitude of the director, this was likely to be in the *more* category.

Careful to keep at the outer edges of activity and well beyond camera range, Gwenn moved through the shadows. She spotted Joyce Hazzlit on the brightly lit set without any trouble. Dressed in a slinky ice-blue satin gown, she was playing one of the diners. She looked aristocratic and not as young as she had appeared in the photograph. Gwenn had no doubts, but she approached a woman she took to be a dresser.

"I'm looking for Joyce Hazzlit. Could you tell me which one she is?"

"The one in blue."

"Thank you."

Next Gwenn moved up to a handsome young man in tuxedo and full makeup, an actor waiting for his scene to be called. "I'm looking for Joyce Hazzlit," she said. "Could you point her out to me?"

"The blonde in blue."

Gwenn asked a couple more times. That should do it, she thought. The word that someone was looking for her should get to Joyce Hazzlit, for sure.

They would be shooting for the rest of the night, she was told. It was a good time to go back to East End Avenue.

At nine P.M. Gwenn Ramadge rang the bell of Joyce Hazzlit's neighbor on the fourth floor, Elton Krauss. There was no response for a considerable time, but she waited. According to the super, Krauss was in his eighties and stayed close to home. If he had gone out, he'd be back soon, she thought. Then the intercom crackled and a voice quavered.

"Who is it?"

"I'm an insurance investigator for Shirer and Smith, the company that manages your building."

"Yes?"

"We're inspecting the building to reassess the insurance coverage. I wonder if I might take a look through your apartment? It'll take just a few minutes."

"At this hour?"

She hadn't taken the hour into consideration. "I apologise, Mr. Krauss. I had some car trouble so I'm running late. I thought rather than get you up early tomorrow . . . but I can come back if you prefer."

"No, no, it's all right. Might as well get it over with, I suppose," Krauss responded. "Come on up."

He met her at his apartment door, a frail, old man shrunken inside baggy tweed pants and a brown cardigan with suede patches at the elbows. In the time it had taken Gwenn to reach the fourth floor, Krauss's misgivings had returned. "Do you have identification?"

"Of course." Gwenn smiled at him and delved into her handbag, found her wallet, and extracted one of her business cards.

"Hart Security and Investigations," he read. "I thought you said you were from Shirer and Smith."

"We've been hired by Shirer and Smith."

She noticed he was watching her lips, so she raised her voice, "If you want to call them and confirm, I have their number right here . . ." Again, she searched through the jumble in her purse. Being small, blonde, and at this moment apparently flustered, Gwenn knew she didn't present a threat. She didn't see anything wrong in playing up to that. "Oh dear, I know I've got it here . . . somewhere . . ."

"Why did they hire you?" Krauss asked.

"Yes!" She pulled a card out and held it up triumphantly. "Would you like me to dial for you? I'd be glad to place the call."

"I asked you why they hired you. What do you want?"

He was very defensive, more than the situation warranted, she thought. "According to our records, you've lived in this building . . ."

"Twenty-six years."

"That's right, twenty-six years. That's a while."

"It certainly is. I've always paid my rent on time and I've never caused any trouble. I'm not doing anything illegal."

"There's no question of that, Mr. Krauss," she reassured him. "May I take a look at your kitchen?"

He hesitated. She thought he was going to say no and

order her to leave, but he sighed finally and wordlessly led the way.

Gwenn looked around. "You could sure use some new appliances, couldn't you? And new cabinets. In fact, you could use a new kitchen."

"Then they'd raise my rent. I don't need that."

So that was it, Gwenn thought. The old man was occupying a rent-controlled apartment and was fearful of eviction. News from the landlord could only be bad. She walked over and put her hand on the old-fashioned steam radiator. "How's the heat? Do you get good heat in the winter?"

"As a matter of fact, yes, we do get good heat."

"Okay." She looked up at the ceiling. "I don't see any signs of dampness. How are you for leaks?"

"Good. Very good. No leaks."

"Well, so far everything appears sound. Your neighbors appear to be satisfied with conditions in their apartments, too. I haven't inspected all of them. Your neighbor on this floor, Ms...." She consulted her book. "Ms. Hazzlit. I haven't been able to catch her at home. Is she away?"

"I don't think so. I spoke to her Monday. In fact, she ran a couple of errands for me. I wasn't feeling so good, a little nausea from my medication. So she went to the market for me and to the post office. She's a real kind lady."

"Married?"

"No."

"But she doesn't live alone."

"What gave you that idea? Sure she lives alone."

"According to the neighbors..." Gwenn let it dangle.

"Some people have nothing better to do than gossip. When she first moved in here Joyce had a steady. Sometimes he stayed over, not often. But that's all done. They broke up."

"Recently?"

"What do you care? What are you up to? Are you trying to get her thrown out of the building? Are you trying to get us both thrown out?"

"No, no, Mr. Krauss, it's nothing like that. I'll be honest with you, I'm not here on behalf of Shirer and Smith. I have nothing to do with them. I made that up so that you'd let me in and talk to me. Ms. Hazzlit's friend is married. I represent his wife."

"In a divorce action?"

"His name is Douglas Trent." She waited for a reaction. "He was murdered about three weeks ago. Maybe you read about it."

Krauss began to shake. He tottered to a chair and, holding on to the arms, lowered himself into it. His color was bad; his breathing erratic.

"Can I get you something? A glass of water?"

He nodded. When she returned he had a couple of pink tablets in his hand. He took them with the water and then leaned back. Gradually, he grew calmer.

"Joyce is so good," he said. "Every day she rings my doorbell and looks in to see that I'm all right and to ask if I need anything. Every single day. One night, right after she'd moved in, I got up and went into the kitchen to make myself a late snack. I fell on the kitchen floor. I couldn't get up. I lay there for seven hours till she found me the next morning. She called 911. She rode in the ambulance with me and waited with me in the emergency room till I was treated and released. If it wasn't for Joyce Hazzlit, I wouldn't be here today. She doesn't deserve this kind of trouble. She certainly didn't deserve the abuse.

"I never said anything to anybody because she didn't want me to, but I cried for her. I cried over what I heard; these walls are thick and my hearing isn't so good, but when he knocked her around, I heard. I heard when he sent her crashing into the furniture or up against a wall. But I never heard a sound out of her, not so much as a whimper. I begged her to go to the police, but she was afraid. I told her to throw him out, but she insisted he was sorry and had promised never to do it again." His rheumy eyes filled. "She made me promise not to tell. He broke his promise, and now I've broken mine."

He had also broken the case.

Gwenn felt no elation. On the contrary, she regretted the pain she was causing the old man, but she was obliged to continue.

Had he ever seen Miss Hazzlit's friend? she wanted to know.

Only through the peephole, Krauss replied.

Would he be able to identify him?

Krauss thought he would, so she showed him a series of photographs among which was a shot of Trent that she'd secured from Rachel Montrone.

"*That's him!*" Krauss had been positive.

Next, Gwenn established that the affair seemed to have ended at about the time Douglas and Emma were married. Joyce had come in to announce that it was over. They'd had a glass of wine together in celebration. The calm lasted for about six months. Then one night she came home after a late shoot to find him sitting on the sofa in her living room and it started all over again. The abuse was worse than ever. Krauss offered to go to the police himself, but she wouldn't let him.

She said she'd take care of it herself.

Things had been quiet lately, Krauss told Gwenn Ramadge, but he was still nervous on behalf of his friend, and still listened for sounds from next door. But so far so good.

How long since the last incident? Gwenn wanted to know.

He couldn't be sure, couldn't fix a date, but it had to

go back to the end of May because Joyce was in Bermuda on a shoot the first week in June.

"When did she get back?"

"The ninth," he replied promptly. "I know because I'd been holding her mail for her."

Since the job had been done by hired killers, that didn't mean much.

"This past Sunday," Gwenn asked, "was she at home?" That was the night Paulie Kellen was shot.

It was obvious that Elton Krauss wanted to help his friend. "Yes, we watched television together."

"Till what time?"

He took a chance. "We watched the eleven o'clock news."

Chapter _____
_____ SEVENTEEN

At seven the next morning, Gwenn Ramadge made what she hoped would be the last phone call but one to the suspect. She didn't expect the model to answer. She waited patiently through the recorded announcement and then the beep to leave her message:

"He wasn't worth spending the rest of your life in jail. Think about it. I'll call again tonight."

She purposely didn't give a specific time. She wanted to keep Joyce Hazzlit off balance, unable to plan any counter attack. Next, she contacted Marge at home before she left for the office. She sent her to the new branch of Beth Israel at Eighty-seventh on East End Avenue. If Joyce Hazzlit had sought treatment after the beatings, logically she would have gone there; it was practically next door.

Finally, she called Ray.

"I need to see you. Can you spare me a few minutes?"

"I'm on my way out, but . . . how soon can you be here?"

"Thirty minutes."

"I'll wait."

Ray Dixon sat her beside his desk, offered coffee which she refused, and then told her to go ahead. He listened without interruption till she was through.

"I don't think she'll buy it," he said. "It was different with the kid. He was in it from the beginning. He'd taken money from her to commit the crime. It couldn't have been a total surprise when he tried to blackmail her. But you . . . you're coming out of left field."

"I've laid a foundation. I've gone to a lot of trouble to make her believe . . ."

"That you're a blackmailer too. Okay, but you also let it be known that you work for Emma Trent."

"I had to."

"But why should Joyce Hazzlit believe you're willing to betray your client?"

"Why not? I've uncovered crucial evidence and I'm trying to sell it to the highest bidder. It's not unheard of. Why should she suspect a trap, particularly when, as you said just now, Paulie had already put the bite on her?"

"All right. Let's say she buys you as a blackmailer. What makes you think she's going to meet you somewhere and hand over a packet of money?"

"I don't expect that. I expect that first she's going to try to find out how much I know, how much of a threat I present."

"And then?"

"We'll play it by ear."

"We?"

"Sure. I don't plan to sit all alone out in the open and wait for her to creep up and shoot me in the back like she did the kid."

"I'm glad to hear that."

"And I don't intend to meet her without backup, either."

"Which you expect me to provide?"

"You will, won't you?"

He started to scowl and then groaned instead. He shook his head. "This whole thing is dramatic and unnecessary. I'll get a search warrant and go through her apartment. Once we have the gun, we test-fire it. If the bullets match those in Kellen's body . . . that's it."

Gwenn bit her lip. "The gun isn't in the apartment." She winced in anticipation of his reaction.

"How do you know?"

"I looked."

"You broke in?"

"Not exactly."

"What does that mean?"

"I was in the building talking to one of her neighbors. He had a key. I borrowed it. It seemed like a good opportunity."

Dixon shook his head. "You know what? You're lucky, Miss Ramadge. Suppose you'd found the gun? What would you have done?"

"I wouldn't have touched it; I know better than that. I would have called you and then you could have got a warrant."

"You could still be charged with tampering with evidence."

"The neighbor, Elton Krauss, says he heard sounds through the walls," Gwenn continued. "He interpreted those sounds according to what Hazzlit told him. He was not a witness to the actual violence. As for Paulie Kellen or Adam McClure, she never mentioned them to him. We can't connect her to them through him. The only chance we have is to take her with the gun in her possession."

"By offering yourself as bait."

"Under controlled circumstances," she pointed out, watching him. He was coming around, she thought.

"No," he decided. "No. It's out of the question. It's too risky."

"I'm not afraid."

"Then you're a fool."

"If I were a policewoman..."

"You're not."

"I'm going to do it, Ray. With or without your help, I'm going to do it. And for your information, I lied just now. I am scared. Real scared. I also realize that what I'm asking is not exactly standard procedure. I don't want you to get into trouble, so forget I mentioned it. You never heard a word about it."

His eyes met hers. "If I get you a Kevlar vest, will you wear it?"

In addition to the bullet-proof vest provided by Ray Dixon, Gwenn was wearing one of the latest, state-of-the-art surveillance devices—a mini tape recorder with a microphone the size of a pinhead disguised as part of a brooch. Dixon, stationed in what once had been a taxi dispatcher's kiosk, was equipped with a receiver that could pull in voices up to three quarters of a mile away. The coming interview would be taped and Dixon could also offer confirmation as a witness. In addition, Gwen carried her S and W Police Special, not in her handbag, where it was difficult to get at, but in the waistband of her slacks. She had told Ray she would arrive at the rendezvous late, after the suspect was already there. In fact, she was early. She parked at the top of a gentle rise from where she could look down on the station and survey the various approaches.

It was primarily a residential area. Cars lined both sides of the streets, bumper to bumper, and would not move till morning. Gillian's Bar was the only commercial establishment open and it was scheduled to close at midnight. She couldn't locate Ray or his people, but she had no doubt they were there. If she couldn't spot them, neither could Joyce Hazzlit. Just then the warning bell clanged announcing an oncoming train and the crossing bars, red lights flashing, came down to block the tracks from both sides. It was 11:09. Gwenn had provided herself with a timetable, but it listed only those trains that made a stop and they were few. This was a through train. It didn't even slow down. In fact, it seemed to her that it gathered speed as it passed through. When it was gone, a solitary figure was standing where there had been no one before.

Gwenn got out of her car, checked the gun in her waistband, then walked down.

The all clear rang, the barrier was raised. The woman crossed.

"Miss Hazzlit?"

"You're the private investigator?"

By the light of the full moon high in the sky, they looked each other over.

Joyce Hazzlit wore jeans and a bulky sweater. A scarf covered her lustrous, silver-blonde hair. Once she had been strikingly beautiful; only last night on the set Gwenn had seen for herself strong indications of her youthful good looks. All traces were now gone. She was haggard and haunted, and the shadows under her eyes were like ugly bruises. The pale hair showed dark roots. She was close to the breaking point, and Gwenn had helped to put her there. It had been part of the plan, yet now she wished she could call it off. She wished she could turn her back and walk away. Then what about Emma?

"I saw you at the funeral," Joyce Hazzlit said. She didn't say whose; it wasn't necessary. "You're not what I expected. Not that it matters. I haven't got ten thousand dollars. If I had, I wouldn't give it to you."

"How much have you got?" Gwenn asked.

"Why should I pay you anything?"

"You were Douglas Trent's lover for at least twelve years. While his first wife lived and during the period of her illness, you took his abuse, his violent abuse, excusing him on the ground that he was undergoing severe emotional strain. That was what he told you when he pleaded for your forgiveness time after time. Isn't that right?"

She didn't answer.

"After her death, you thought he'd change. You expected he'd ask you to marry him. Neither of these things happened; he continued to abuse you and he didn't mention marriage. No, in fact, he went and married someone else. I have a witness who will testify the affair began before Lucille's death and continued after. It stopped abruptly when he married Emma Trent. About six months later, he started seeing you again. I have Douglas Trent's personal appointment calendar in which his dates with you are noted in his own hand. Once I turn the book over to the police, they'll interrogate your neighbors. I doubt Trent could have gone in and out of your building over that period of time without being noticed. Mr. Krauss might be prepared to lie for you, but I doubt any of the others would." Gwenn paused.

"All right, we had an affair. It did start while his first wife was alive and resumed after he married a second time." She shrugged. "He just couldn't stay away."

"And you took him back?"

"Yes."

"But the violence continued as before. In fact, it got worse."

"That's not true. He didn't hit me anymore."

Which was an admission of sorts, Gwenn thought. "Records from Beth Israel North's emergency room show the dates you went in for treatment and what your injuries were. The resident physician in charge on one such occasion wrote up in his notes that he suspected domestic violence but that you refused to file a police complaint."

"The doctor was mistaken."

The clang of the crossing bell interrupted. Gwenn was silent while the barrier arms went down. This train slowed as it pulled into the station and stopped. Only

the conductor got out. He looked up and down the platform, blew his whistle to signal the all clear to the engineer, and got back on. The train started and slowly
glided out of the station. As soon as the last car cleared
the crossing, the bell rang and the arms went up.

"You were afraid to go to the police," Gwenn picked
up where she'd left off. "You were afraid of what Douglas
would do to you. But you couldn't take any more abuse.
You realized at last that your lover's behavior was a
perversion of passion and he wouldn't stop till he ended
up killing you. Your only resource was to kill him first."

A light wind rose. Gwenn sensed a stirring of the shrubbery behind her. A cloud passed over the moon, casting
both platforms and the two women into deep shadow.

"You went out and bought a gun, a small, neat .22."
Gwen was going on instinct now, feeling her way. "But
you didn't have the courage to use it." She sensed rather
than saw Joyce Hazzlit's reaction, felt the tension. "You
had to hire somebody to do the job for you. You found
Paulie Kellen. You chose him because he was an addict,
and he agreed to do the job because he needed money
to support his habit. What you didn't take into account
was that addicts never have enough money and that he
would come back to blackmail you. And keep coming
back."

"You have a vivid imagination, Miss Ramadge. Where's
your proof? Have you one shred of evidence to support
any of this?"

"Not in my possession."

Joyce Hazzlit shook her head in exasperation. "Who
has it? What is it? Put up or shut up, Miss Ramadge."

"It exists," Gwenn said with complete assurance. If
she could break Hazzlit on the Kellen murder, and she
now believed she could, all the rest would follow. "You
came close to committing the perfect crime. You have no
idea how I analyzed and agonized before finding the weak

link. It was the hired killer, of course. You thought your secret was safe with him; he couldn't betray you without betraying himself. But Kellen made a deal with the district attorney by turning over his friend, Adam. He might even improve it by turning you over. So he could blackmail you with impunity. As long as he lived, he would be a threat to you.

"So when Paulie Kellen made his demand, you pretended to give in. You arranged to meet him here with the money. He came. You were late, purposely. He sat on that bench and waited. You crept up behind him and shot him in the back with the gun you'd bought to kill your lover. You shot him with the gun you have right now in your purse. You had courage enough for that."

Joyce Hazzlit's sigh seemed to come from the very depths of her being. It suggested resignation. Or was it relief? "You mean this one?" Suddenly the gun was in her hand and pointed at Gwenn.

Gwenn stood very still. She made no attempt to go for her own weapon. She had no wish to exchange fire. She was protected by a bullet proof vest. The woman who confronted her was not.

"You should have gotten rid of it," she said. "You can't use it. The bullets will match those recovered from Paulie Kellen's body. Shooting me with that gun will be like putting your signature to a confession."

A harsh gust of wind rustled the leaves, made stinging whirlpools of dust and drove the clouds from the face of the moon. Once again, the station was bathed in the cold clarity of its light. Joyce Hazzlit stood spotlighted. Her face was tranquil, the deep furrows smoothed, the ugly shadows gone. Her head scarf slipped off and her silver-blonde hair cast an aura around her.

"I'm sorry about the boy, Adam." Her voice was low, filled with regret. "I know how he must have felt. He got dragged into it through no fault of his own. I'm sorry about the other one too, Paulie. He was corrupted long before I met him, but I took advantage. I used him. I wish I hadn't." Her eyes filled. The gun trembled in her hand.

"I don't feel any regret for Douglas. He abused, degraded, and humiliated me. He let me think that after Lucille's death he would marry me. Instead, he married a woman he'd just met. After the initial shock, I realized I was lucky. I was free. I didn't need to be afraid anymore. I didn't need to jump when the phone rang—it wouldn't be Douglas to say he was on the way over. I didn't need to wince when someone raised a hand; it wouldn't be a slap or a blow. Months went by. Six good months. Then one night I came home and there he was— sitting on the couch in my living room, waiting for me. He still had the keys to the apartment, of course; it had never occurred to me to change the locks. Not that it would have mattered, he would have got in somehow. Anyway, it all started up again. That same night, he broke my arm in two places. Within two months I got pregnant. He kicked me in the stomach. I had a miscarriage."

Gwenn could only shake her head.

"That was when I made up my mind to kill him. I went out and got a gun, but, you're right, I didn't have the guts to use it. Oh, I tried. I actually did try. The very next time he came at me, I pulled the gun. I pointed it straight at him. He laughed. He laughed and slapped it out of my hand. And then he punched and kicked me worse than ever before. He hit me where it would show. I couldn't go out of the house for a week. It was over three weeks before I could work. And he didn't even bother to take the gun away. He left it where it fell when he knocked it out of my hand—on the kitchen floor."

To show his utter contempt, Gwenn thought.

"I realized then that I'd never be able to do it myself."

She bowed her head. "But where was I going to find somebody to do it for me?" She paused as though she expected Gwenn to provide the answer. "It was Douglas himself who showed me where to look.

"He was constantly complaining about the time Emma spent at the dance school. He resented that she had her own career and was successful. He hinted she was making out with the boys. I don't know if he really believed that."

Of course! Gwenn recalled Emma's account of the encounter in the studio: how Trent had slapped her around and taken her money and then how her husband and young McClure passed each other on the stairs. That chance encounter might have fired his obsession. For Joyce to have had to listen to his ravings over Emma must have been the ultimate humiliation.

"Did he mention a specific name? Did he accuse one particular student?"

"More than one, oh, believe me. I went to the basketball game to look them over and chose the biggest and the strongest."

"That was Paulie Kellen?" Gwenn prompted.

"Yes. I was very careful in making the approach. I asked around about him. I found out he was involved with drugs. He had a reputation as a bully. When it came time to meet, it was his idea to come here, in this place. I wore a dark wig and used dark makeup. I didn't tell him my name and I paid in cash. I told him he might need someone to go with him, to help. They should make it look like a burglary, I told him. They should beat Douglas like he beat me."

And Emma, Gwenn thought.

"I went to Douglas's funeral. He wouldn't have gone to mine. I saw him interred. I watched them shovel the dirt on his casket. I thought it was over at last. I thought I could forget and start a new life. And then, somehow, Paulie Kellen found me."

She was silent for a long time. "Even if I'd paid what he wanted, that wouldn't have been the end of it." She stared at Gwenn. "If I pay you, what guarantee do I have that you won't be back for more?"

Her hand was steady as she raised the gun.

A scream formed in Gwenn's throat, but fear paralyzed her vocal cords.

Neither of them heard the approaching train.

Suddenly, instead of aiming at Gwenn, Joyce Hazzlit turned the gun to her own head.

"No!"

Desperation ripped the scream free and Gwenn crouched to take a flying tackle in order at least to divert her aim. Anticipating, Joyce Hazzlit spun to the right, left leg reaching out past the edge of the platform, and fell to the tracks just as the train entered the station. It was a through train going at full speed.

The engineer braked fast, but before he could bring the train to a halt, three cars had passed over the body. Gwenn was paralyzed; she couldn't even turn her head away. Ray Dixon and his team came out of the shadows only to watch helplessly. It took a while before the clank of the wheels and the hissing of brakes was absorbed into silence, a silence in which time itself seemed suspended. Then, in the distance, sirens wailed. Various rescue units began to arrive: ES, EMS, police, fire trucks. The small station was overrun. Windows in the surrounding buildings were thrown open and people leaned dangerously far out. Some of the residents even came down into the street. On the train, passengers congregated on the exit platforms, but the doors remained closed.

"Are you all right?" Dixon asked Gwenn.

She nodded. In the way he meant, yes, but . . . emotionally she was badly shaken.

There was a standard procedure for handling this kind

of violent death, which involved both police and fire departments. It had already been set in motion and its own momentum would carry it through to conclusion. In fact, at that very moment the train whistle sounded twice and slowly, very slowly, the train started to back up: the first step in the retrieval of the body had begun.

Dixon gave Gwenn a searching look. "Wait for me," he said and then went to join the ES unit as they walked out on the tracks.

Photographs were taken. An assistant ME made a brief examination, then the remains were carefully placed in a body bag and strapped to a gurney. It didn't take long. There was no one to question. Aside from Gwenn, the witnesses were Dixon himself and the detectives with him. He sent them back to the squad and returned to Gwenn. She looked a little better, but not much.

"You'll have to make a statement and sign it, but it can wait till morning."

"Thanks."

"I'll take you home now."

"You don't need to. I have my car."

"You're in no condition to drive."

"I'm fine. I can drive."

"Okay, you can drive. Do you want to?"

She bit her lip. "No."

It was close to midnight when they got to her place. Dixon was able to park right in front of the building. He accompanied her upstairs to her door. She handed him the key and let him go in and turn on the lights and hang up her coat for her.

"How about I make us both some hot tea and maybe you have something bracing to put into it?"

"I'll do it."

He started to argue and then changed his mind. "Okay." He settled himself on the sofa.

His agreeing so readily surprised her, but she didn't say so and in due course she set out the tea tray along with a bottle of Drambuie. "Will this do?"

"Couldn't be better." He picked up the bottle and poured a generous amount of the liqueur in each cup. They sipped. Dixon waited as it coursed down his throat and its warmth spread through his whole body, till he saw that Gwenn felt it, too.

"Joyce Hazzlit meant to kill herself. It was not an accident," he told her. "Her foot didn't slip. She deliberately stepped off the platform. You were not responsible."

Gwenn's green eyes widened. "How did you know?"

"That you were blaming yourself?" He reached for her hand. "Your compassion shows."

"If ever a murder was justified ..."

"No." He cut her off sharply. "There was intense provocation, I grant you, but she not only got Trent killed, she turned two teenage boys into murderers. Don't ever forget that."

"But I tricked her into confessing. That bothers me."

"It shouldn't. Paulie Kellen threatened her and you re-created that situation. She would have killed you, too, except that you showed her she couldn't get away with it."

True; it was at that point that Joyce Hazzlit had changed, Gwenn recalled. She had seemed almost relieved, as though the decision had been taken out of her hands. Could that have been when she chose to turn the gun on herself? Gwenn sighed and sipped some more of the hot drink. Suddenly, she put the cup down. "How did the boys know that Douglas Trent would be home alone on that Wednesday night?"

Dixon frowned. "I suppose ... she called and told them. She gave them the go-ahead. We've been through all that."

"How did she know? She was in Bermuda."

"They have phones in Bermuda."

"But how did she know? Who told her?"

"Trent. Maybe he called and told her."

"Why?"

"Why not?"

Gwenn thought about it. "No reason. I suppose he might have. He probably did keep tabs on her, but ... how could she have known Emma wouldn't be there?"

"Damn it, Gwenn! She confessed to soliciting the Kellen kid. She was in possession of the gun that killed him and admitted that, too. Your client is exonerated on all counts. What more do you want?"

"Nothing."

"So forget about it, okay? Get a good night's sleep." He leaned over and kissed her cheek lightly. "You'll feel better in the morning."

But she didn't. Though she slept the night through without interruption, she was still tired when she got up. And depressed. She didn't feel like going to work. She had to drag herself to the office.

Marge Pratt looked up eagerly when she walked in and saw right away congratulations were not in order. "I guess you feel bad about what happened."

Gwenn had not expected her to be so sensitive. "Yes, I do."

"It was her choice," Marge pointed out. "I think she made up her mind before meeting with you that if you had hard evidence against her, she'd put an end to it."

It seemed everyone had figured it out, Gwenn thought.

"Anyhow, it clears Mrs. Trent and that's what we were hired to do. You've got to feel good about that."

"Have you been talking to Sergeant Dixon?"

"No." Marge didn't understand why Gwenn asked.

She dismissed it. "Should I get Mrs. Trent on the phone for you?"

"Later."

Gwenn passed into her office and closed the door behind her. She took off her jacket, sat at her desk, and swiveled the chair around to face the window and leaned back. She picked up where she and Ray had left off the night before. She didn't want to. He had told her to leave it alone, to be satisfied, and now Marge had said the same thing. But there was that one question remaining. Maybe it wasn't any more than a loose end, but until she had an answer to it, she couldn't rest.

Assume Douglas Trent had called Joyce in Bermuda and mentioned he was going home a day early. Fine. How could she have known that Emma Trent wouldn't be there?

And there was another loose end—the bats used to beat Trent. Where had they been hidden between the night of the murder and the night of the attempted burning? She knew only what Lew and Ray had told her. It might help to see the official report. Lew was still in Miami, but by now she had no hesitation in contacting Ray.

"It strikes me as odd that the boys took the bats away with them," she explained. "The bats were soaked in Trent's blood. Wherever they put them, they must have left a mark. They would have been better off to leave them at the scene."

"You're talking like they were pros. They're only kids. They were only kids," he corrected himself.

"What exactly did the man who saw the bonfire say?"

"I'll read it to you."

She would have liked to see the report for herself, but this would do for now. "Go ahead."

He read the part comprising the witness's description

of the scene and his glimpse of the perpetrator. He read it slowly, in a flat tone, without emphasis. When he was finished, he waited for her comment.

She made none.

"I told you there was nothing in it."

"Would you mind if I talked to Mr. Bates?"

"Are you onto something?"

"I'm not sure. I'd like to confirm the description of the perp that Mr. Bates gave."

"He couldn't give a description; he was too far away."

"He says he could make out a silhouette against the flames: medium height, slight build."

"So?"

"Both Kellen and McClure were big boys, close to seven feet. Basketball players."

Ray groaned.

They got to the supermarket at four that afternoon. Jerry Bates had just started his shift and was in the basement checking stock. His skin was pasty and he was over-weight, but there was something about him as he approached, a presence, that impressed them. It was part of his stage training, though they didn't know that. His dark eyes darted from one to the other. He was excited, eager to help, but it seemed he couldn't add anything to his original statement.

"I was at least fifty yards away and the kid was in deep among the trees. I could barely make him out by the light of the fire." He sighed. "I'm sorry."

"How do you know it was a kid?" Gwenn asked. "Couldn't it have been an adult?"

It had been an instinctive conclusion, Bates realized and tried to explain. "There was something about him ...about his build. He was medium height, and he ran like a kid."

"Are you sure about his height?" Gwenn asked.

"He was hunched over the fire, but when I yelled he straightened up and froze for a second before he turned and bolted. I'd say he was five foot five or six, no more."

Gwenn and Ray exchanged looks.

"Could it have been a woman?" Ray asked as casually as he could.

Bates closed his eyes to bring up the scene on the screen of his mind. "He was wearing a dark jogging outfit and he had a baseball cap pulled way down over his eyes." Then, using the empathy of an actor, the witness re-created the emotion he had sensed in the fire starter. Near panic, out of proportion to the moment he had thought then, and did so again now. "It could have been," he told the detectives. "It could have been a woman."

They thanked Jeremiah Bates and came up from the cool dampness of the cellar into bright, hot sunshine. Gwenn shivered.

"Joyce Hazzlit was in Bermuda. It wasn't her."

Early on, Gwenn had sensed that the overnight hiding place of the bats would prove vital. Then they hadn't known where to look. Now they did. The bats, of course, would no longer be there, but they would have left traces. For the second time in the case, blood would tell.

For once she was content to let Ray set up the operation. And he was meticulous about keeping her informed. Neither wanted to risk a mistake. They had one chance, only one.

Gwenn went to see her client the next afternoon.

Emma grasped her hand warmly. "The charges have been dropped. I owe it all to you."

Gwenn hesitated a moment before taking it. "You're going away, you said?"

"Yes, for a couple of months." She'd noted Gwenn's

reluctance. "I'll travel through Europe. No set schedule or itinerary. If I like a place, I'll stay, and if I don't I'll move on."

"And then?"

"I don't know. I'll sell this house, that's for sure. I don't want to live here anymore."

"I understand. Well, I won't keep you. There are just a couple of loose ends."

"Anything at all, Gwenn. May I call you Gwenn? Just ask." She led the way into the living room. Today, the drapes were open, showing on the garden and past it, the empty street.

"How long were you aware your husband had a mistress?" Gwenn asked.

The smile was quickly gone. "I didn't know. I had no idea. I was stunned to learn of it."

"And when was that? When Miss Hazzlit came to see you?"

"She never came to see me." Emma Trent appeared perplexed.

"Of course she did. She was jealous of you. That's understandable. After all the years she'd given him, you were the one Douglas Trent married. She was curious about you. She wanted to see what you had to offer that she didn't. Why you should be the one living happily ever after instead of her. She came out here hoping to catch a glimpse of you, only that. Then, when she saw you, the moment she laid eyes on you, she knew Douglas was treating you the same way he had treated her. She didn't have a moment's doubt and on impulse she walked up to you and introduced herself. There was instant empathy between you."

"Where did you get this crazy idea?"

"Not from Joyce," Gwenn assured her. "She never spoke your name. She went to her death in silence."

Relief was followed by satisfaction and then that, too, was wiped away. "What are you after?"

"The truth, finally. You and Joyce Hazzlit were accomplices. Trent had abused you both and together you intended to get revenge. You hatched the plot so that each would be responsible for only a part. You selected who should do the job. You chose Paulie Kellen because you knew he was an addict and he had a reputation for violence, but it was Joyce who contacted him, made the deal, and paid him. Paul recruited Adam. Adam did whatever his friend wanted. In this instance he would also be helping you, but he had no idea you were knowingly involved. Neither of the boys knew.

"Joyce's Bermuda booking was providential. If she hadn't been offered the job, she would have had to find some excuse to be away. You, of course, had to be here—to discover the body, to notify the police, to answer their questions. To play the part of the grieving widow. It was also up to you to decide when the murder should be done."

"What do you want?" Emma Trent's lovely face hardened; her amber eyes narrowed. "How much?"

"Besides Douglas's secretary, you were the only one who knew he was coming home a day early. You knew because you called Canada every day to find out. Finally, on Wednesday, you got the news you wanted. He was on his way. You called Paulie Kellen, disguising your voice, and told him to go ahead. That night you conducted your regular late class and then, while the boys were entering your house, you went around the corner to the movies, making sure to be seen by as many people as possible when you came out.

"Douglas had come home to an empty house. The boys were waiting outside. As soon as he went in, they went in—through the back as arranged by Joyce. They were instructed to blow the safe, but they were not instructed to take anything. That was an oversight. The sound of the explosion reached Douglas in the upstairs bedroom and he came out to see what was going on. The boys were on the way up. They met on the landing. Wielding the bats, they backed him into the room and clubbed him to his knees.

"All as planned. They did what they'd been told. You were the one who made the mistake."

"What mistake?"

"When the police questioned you, you told them that as you approached the house you saw light in the upstairs window. You entered and called up to your husband. When he didn't answer, you went directly upstairs. You were shocked and sickened by what you saw. You threw up and stumbled out to your own room down the hall and called 911 from there."

"That's right."

"Not quite. You were sickened and you did throw up, but you didn't run out and make the call, not then. You took your time to look around and to make sure everything was as it should be, and that was when you saw the two bats lying on the floor. You assumed the boys would have taken them away. You thought those blood-soaked bats would be a clear and direct lead back to the boys, and any clue to them would put you at risk."

Gwenn paused. Emma Trent, outwardly calm, waited.

"You didn't know whether the police would search the house, or how thoroughly, but you couldn't leave those bats there in plain sight. You had to hide them at least temporarily."

"What's your point?"

"You got them out of the house and then you called 911." Gwenn stole a look at her watch, then suddenly closed her eyes. "May I have some water?"

Emma Trent stared at her. "Are you sick?"

"It's nothing. If I could have some water, please?"

From beneath her hand, Gwenn watched as Emma Trent crossed the hall into the dining room and passed through to the kitchen. She strained to listen to every sound in the house and out in the street. Then Emma Trent was back. Gwenn took the glass and drank deeply.

"What are we waiting for?" Emma Trent asked.

"We're waiting for the police to arrive and to conduct the search they should have conducted on the night of the murder."

As though on a signal, the front doorbell rang.

Ray Dixon and two uniforms stood on the threshold. "I have a search warrant, Mrs. Trent. It covers the house, the grounds, the garage, and all the contents thereof. We'll start with the garage. Is it locked?"

"No."

"How about the car?"

"The keys are on a hook beside the kitchen door."

"You may come with us, if you want, Mrs. Trent."

"I'll stay here."

"So will I," Gwenn said.

Dixon's look was stern. "And so will Officer Sorbino."

Gwenn flushed.

They weren't gone long. When Ray returned, he was carrying a section of gray carpeting.

"This comes from the trunk of your car," he told Emma. "We'll be taking it with us." He handed her a receipt.

She took it without a word.

"As you can see, there's a dark stain in this corner. The lab will analyze it. If it's blood, the same blood that was on the bats, your husband's blood..." He left it hanging.

"Then what?" she challenged. She looked from Ray to Gwenn and back again. "That's all you've got?"

"It will be enough," Gwenn promised.

"Don't be too sure," she retorted. "I'm not going to oblige you by confessing. I'm not going to blow the top of my head off or jump in front of a train. I'm not afraid to go into court. I'll take the stand. When the jury hears what Douglas did and what he was, who do you think they're going to feel sorry for? Me, that's who. And Joyce. And the boys, too. He's responsible for their deaths. He was the culprit and he got what he deserved. When I'm through, there won't be any doubt about that. I'm not a quitter like Joyce. I'm going to fight to my last breath."

A slight smile made the corners of her mouth twitch. "Remember, I have a very good lawyer. I can thank you for that, Miss Ramadge."

"You as good as invited her to make a break for it," Dixon charged. "When I heard you ask for a glass of water, I nearly jumped out of my skin. How could you do that? What got into you? It wasn't part of the plan."

"I know. It came to me suddenly that if she made a break, it would be as good as a confession. Wouldn't it?"

He groaned.

The arrest had been made. The suspect waited in the holding cell for her attorney. Gwenn had completed and signed her statement. Now she sat beside Ray's desk in the squad room. It was the first private and relatively quiet moment they'd had.

"I knew you were out there and I knew she wouldn't get past you."

He shook his head at her. "Being a PI doesn't give you the right to make your own rules or to work outside the law. You haven't the right to make judgments any more than we do."

"I realize that. I'm sorry."

"It's a bad habit."

"Yes, I know. Very bad."

"It's not a good idea to get personally involved."

"No, it isn't."

"Well . . . okay." He wound down lamely. "How about dinner?"

"Lew's back. He left a message he'd be calling."

"Oh? I hadn't heard. That must mean his father's okay."

"Yes." She got up. "I guess we won't be seeing much of each other." She held out her hand. "Thank you for your help."

"No thanks necessary." He took her hand and held it for a long time before letting it go.

He didn't walk her to the door, but when Gwenn turned he was still standing and looking at her.

Lew didn't call till late, and then he was ill at ease. "I'm sorry. I've been meaning to get in touch, but I've had so much to do."

"I see." She didn't, but what else was there to say? "How's your father?"

"Better. Much better. They're going to release him at the end of next week."

"That's wonderful news. I'm glad, Lew."

"Thanks." He swallowed. "Could we talk? I don't mean on the phone. I need to see you. Tomorrow?"

"Of course. Dinner? I'll fix something."

"I'll come tomorrow, but I can't stay for dinner."

"Why not? What's the matter, Lew?"

"Is seven okay? I'll be there at seven." He hung up.

Lew arrived promptly. He brought her flowers and turned down the offer of a drink. She took the flowers, but he didn't even wait for her to put them in water.

"I'm moving to Miami."

They stood in the middle of her living room facing each other, Gwenn with the bouquet still in her hands.

"My father is very sick."

"I thought you said he was better."

"He's well enough to get out of the hospital, but he can't take care of himself. I don't want to put him in a nursing home. He wouldn't like it and I can't afford it."

She was beginning to see where he was headed.

"I thought of bringing him up here to live with me, but he'd be home alone all day and a lot of nights too. He'd need a full-time attendant," he went on. The strain of the recent days at his father's bedside was evident in his haggard face and the slump of his shoulders. "Down there, he has friends and neighbors who can look in on him. He's comfortable with his surroundings. It's easier for me to make the move than it is for him. I can get a job on the local force or in private security, if it comes to that. No problem."

"I see."

He took a deep breath. "I don't suppose you'd like to live in Miami? You could come down and visit. Try it. See how you like it."

In his eyes she saw a reflection of the companionship they'd shared in their work, the friendship, the laughter. She searched his face and found a tenderness he'd never let her see before, and passion that he'd kept hidden because it was how she'd wanted it. She was deeply touched and for a moment regretted they hadn't gone farther. Should she say yes now?

"I don't think so, Lew," she murmured gently.

"You could open an office down there."

"It wouldn't work," she said, even more gently.

He sighed, took a half step toward her, then stopped. "It's too much. I shouldn't have asked. I'm sorry."

"Don't be sorry. I'm not." Closing the distance between them, she reached up on tiptoe and kissed him.

Gwenn put the flowers in a vase and placed them on the hall console. Then she went into the kitchen. It was going to be another soup and crackers night. She got a can of minestrone out of the cupboard, emptied it into a pot, and put that on the stove. She set a place at the kitchen table and popped a couple of slices of whole wheat bread into the toaster because she was out of crackers. The phone rang.

"Hi. It's me, Ray."

"Yes, Ray, what is it?"

"Have you eaten?"

"As a matter of fact, I was just fixing..."

"Don't. I'll take you out. I know a great place right in your neighborhood."

"I don't think so, Ray, thanks. By the time you get here..."

"I'm across the street. By the time you get your coat, I'll be at the door." He hung up.

Moments later the downstairs bell rang and Gwenn buzzed him in. Moments after that, her doorbell rang. Ray Dixon stood on the threshold with a big smile and a bunch of spring flowers, which he handed her with a flourish. "You haven't got your coat on. Or is it too warm for a coat?"

"What's going on?" Gwenn indicated the flowers on the console. "I haven't received this many flowers since my graduation. What were you doing across the street? Were you waiting for Lew to leave? How did you know he was here?"

"He told me he was coming."

"Why should he do that?"

"Because I was the one who told him to come to see you. He's quitting the force and moving to Florida to look after his father. He didn't think it was fair to ask you to marry him when it meant taking on such a burden. I said he should give you the option. Let you make the decision." He waited for her reaction. "He did ask you, didn't he?"

"In a way."

"Good." Ray was relieved, then worried again. "You did turn him down? When I saw Lew leave I assumed..."

"You have no right to assume anything."

"All I did..."

"You meddled. You have no right to meddle in my private affairs."

"I'm sorry."

"You have a tendency to do that, you know." Her eyes fixed on his. "It's a bad habit."

"Yes, I know. Very bad."

"Right." She nodded briskly. "So, I'll just put these in water and we can go." When she had arranged the flowers to her satisfaction, she took a light raincoat from the closet. As Ray helped her into it, she looked around at him.

"Why did you push Lew to propose?"

"If he hadn't asked, you'd never have known what your answer would have been."

"Suppose I'd said yes?"

"It was a chance I had to take."